FORGIVENESS

FORGIVENESS

A Novel

JERRY ZINN

Published by Inscript Books
a division of Dove Christian Publishers
P.O. Box 611
Bladensburg, MD 20710-0611
www.inscriptpublishing.com

Inscript and the portrayal of a pen with script are trademarks of Dove Christian Publishers.

Book Design by Mark Yearnings

ISBN: 978-1-957497-14-3

Seven years ago, either a vision from God or just a dream, the ideas and details of the story in this book became very clear to me. I first wrote a movie script that is still waiting to be produced. This story is based on that movie script. My wife, Kathie, began the book from my first writing of the script that was rewritten several times and it was her encouragement that led me to write this heart-warming story of forgiveness. God certainly has a way of working in our lives. May all those who read this book experience the presence of God as I did as I wrote it.

I sincerely thank my wife Kathie for her many hours of typing, her input in the story and her encouragement for me to complete the book. A special thanks also to Carolyn Erickson for her writing and editing ideas, and to Jaffe for his sketch of the cover.

Jerry Zinn

CHAPTER ONE

*I*t was a beautiful April morning in the small southern California town of Beaumont. The aroma of spring flowers and the chirping of various birds only added to this clear, crisp early morning. It was to be a special day for Andrew Hilderbrand. His parents would be returning from their annual business trip to Atlanta, where they met with Eastern representatives of Hilderbrand Enterprises. Also, his high school sweetheart, Jennie Summers, would be returning home from UCSD, where she had just received her degree in Marine Biology. Andrew hadn't seen Jennie in nearly a month, and they were looking forward to discussing plans for their wedding in the very near future. Although excited to be with Jennie, Andrew was wondering why Jennie had chosen not to stay for the commencement exercises.

This morning, Andrew jogged at his usual fast pace, dressed in jogging shorts and his favorite 'Running with Jesus' T-shirt. Sweating profusely and nearly out of breath, he stopped briefly when an elderly couple who had retired from Hilderbrand Enterprises flagged him down.

"How have you been, Andrew?"

"I am fine," Andrew replied, "but I've been busy filling in for Dad while he and Mom were in Atlanta."

"Oh, when do they get home?"

"They are scheduled to arrive home late this afternoon. Good to see you again. You folks have a nice day."

Andrew continued his five-mile jog, thinking about all he had to discuss with his father. His father, Nathan, was the son of Hilderbrand Enterprises founder and owner CJ Hilderbrand. Nathan was the CEO of the company of over 4000 employees. Hilderbrand Enterprises manufactured industrial equipment and supplies and was located on the outskirts of Moreno Valley, just a short drive from Beaumont.

Arriving at his apartment near the edge of town, he sat down on the front step to relax and cool down after his run. Andrew always relished these early morning runs just to reflect and think about the upcoming daily activities. His workload was always more complex when his father was traveling. Filling his father's shoes was a challenge. The best part was that it gave him more opportunities to work alongside his grandfather.

It had always been the tradition for Andrew to meet with his parents at his apartment after their arrival from Atlanta. The reason for this location and not his parents' home Andrew never quite figured out and never questioned that decision. Andrew lived closer to the airport than his parents, and his apartment was right on the way to his parents' home.

In preparation for their return and his anticipated meeting with Jennie, Andrew had tidied up his apartment the day before. That did not require much extra effort because Andrew, unlike many men, had kept his apartment spotless and ready for company, although simply furnished. Andrew was especially proud of two large wall pictures, one of his father and himself and the other of his grandfather. Both pictures displayed them in their baseball uniforms. Baseball had always been an important part of their lives.

Upon getting orange juice from the refrigerator and gulping it down, he undressed and entered the shower. He then proceeded to sing 'When the Roll is Called Up Yonder.' Andrew, not being overly religious as his parents and grandparents, had always favored this special old hymn. It was also his Grandpa CJ's favorite old hymn. Andrew often heard him singing it in his office while at work. He often wondered how the many Hilderbrand employees appreciated CJ's singing Christian music in the office. Unlike the rest of his family, whose voices equaled choir angels in heaven, Andrew's singing was usually off-key.

Before showering, Andrew had turned on the TV, which was airing *Good Morning America*. While in the shower, he was oblivious to a news bulletin that was being broadcast by KTLC, the local news channel. KTLC had interrupted the scheduled programming:

"Nathan Hilderbrand and his wife Louise were struck by an automobile upon entering a crosswalk in downtown Atlanta. Details of the accident are not clear at this moment. KTLC will update the details of this tragic loss as they become available. Nathan was a pillar of his community and was the only son of billionaire CJ Hilderbrand, a lifetime resident of Beaumont and owner of Hildebrand Enterprises. Nathan and his wife have one son, Andrew, 26, an heir apparent to Hildebrand Enterprises."

Andrew had gotten the call about his parents; it was on his answering machine, but he had not checked it when he arrived home from his jog.

After getting out of the shower and dressing, he turned off the TV. His phone started ringing, and he hurried to the phone, expecting a call from Jennie with details of their plans for the day.

"Andrew, are you watching the local news? I'm on my way to your house. Oh, Andrew!"

Andrew frowned and said, "Why?" But Jennie had turned off her phone.

He called CJ and Sara, but there was no answer. Five minutes later, Jennie arrived and ran to Andrew, hugging him close. At about the same time, Andrew's grandparents arrived looking as white as a ghost. Andrew invited them all in. By the looks of the faces on the recent arrivals, he now suspected something had recently occurred, which was causing some real concern.

"What's wrong? Has someone been shot? A fire? What's going on?"

CJ motioned to Jennie to turn the TV on to the local news channel. There was to be a news update at 9:15 a.m.

"It's your father and mother." CJ hugged Andrew, broke down, and couldn't finish. They all sat and stared at the screen, listening.

"This is Matthew Ellsberg reporting for KTLC. We now have details of the fatal accident that took the lives of Louise and Nathan Hilderbrand earlier this morning in Atlanta. The accident occurred at 10:17 a.m. Eastern time, and the car that struck and killed them was driven by 72-year-old Philip Clemmons. It has been confirmed that Clemmons had a massive heart attack while driving in downtown Atlanta and the car he was driving struck and killed the Hilderbrands. Both were killed on impact, dying instantly at the scene. The Hilderbrands have been pillars of the community of Beaumont and have provided employment for 4000 employees in the Beaumont and surrounding communities. Nathan Hilderbrand was the CEO of Hilderbrand Enterprises and is survived by his father CJ, mother, Sara, and son Andrew. Nathan was 52 years old. Again, Nathan and Louise Hilderbrand were struck down and killed in an auto accident earlier this morning while on a business vacation in Atlanta. This is Matthew Ellsberg reporting for KTLC."

Andrew, pale and speechless, turned off the TV. Everyone sat in silence.

After a while, Andrew asked his grandfather, "Grandpa, you are a very religious person. How or why would God allow this to happen to such strong believers? They both have been there for so many with needs in our community. They both have been active and strong supporters of the church. Why, why, why did this happen? How could God have allowed this?"

CJ responded, "I can't answer that. God sometimes allows things to happen, some good and some bad, but who are we to question God? One thing I do know, both Nathan and Louise are in a much better place now than before, and both are now looking down from heaven. We have all been hurt today, and we have lost loved ones. You, Andrew, have lost a mother and father who loved you very much. I have lost my only remaining son and his lovely wife. I know it is going to be difficult, but we all must move forward with our lives and trust that God will provide us with wisdom and eventual understanding. The healing process may take some time, but we must continue to be strong. God will get us through this, and we must remember that God's word tells us that 'nothing can separate us from the love of God.' He will always be with us."

"I know you're right, but I'm not sure I can handle God

right now. He could have prevented this. I just don't understand why so many God-loving Christians are taken so suddenly like this and evil people survive and prosper," Andrew exclaimed. Andrew paced around the room and finally began to sob and pound on the table. At this point, all four of them began to cry. Finally, Andrew walked out of the apartment and started jogging down the street.

"Andrew, wait," Jennie hollered. "Where are you going? I will go with you."

"No, Jennie, Andrew needs some time alone," admonished CJ. "Losing his father, his best friend, and his mother so suddenly will be difficult and will take time for him to heal. They were so close, as were Nathan and I. Nathan was my right-hand man at Hilderbrand Enterprises, and we also discussed company decisions together. Andrew and his father were instrumental in getting little league baseball started in Beaumont. They attended nearly every high school varsity game together. Louise and Sara were so active in the church. She and Sara were involved in the community and were inseparable from any activity involving our church. They team-taught our young adult Sunday School class. Yes, the Hildebrand family, as well as the community of Beaumont, has lost and will miss two wonderful Christian people. Don't bother with funeral questions, Jennie. Sara and I will take care of everything. We will have the bodies flown back here and make all the necessary arrangements."

***

Andrew, running and sweating profusely, panted and called out loud, "Why Lord, why me, what have I done to deserve this? Mother and Father didn't deserve this." Andrew did not realize what was going on around him and continued jogging, paying no attention to those who were waving at him. After his run, Andrew returned to his quiet apartment. Jennie and his grandparents were gone.

After a few days of mourning, Andrew realized that he must return to the office. He suspected that his responsibilities would be increased. Passing by CJ's office, he noticed CJ was in, and he decided to drop in and ask some questions. "What do we do now? Father was the CEO of Hilderbrand Enterprises. You and he were the lifeblood of the company. We all counted on him to run the company, put out fires, and inspire the employees. We don't have anyone capable of taking his place. He was the heart and soul of the company. Our employees and customers respected him and relied on his decisions."

CJ responded, "Andrew, as I recall, you are now 26 years old. Your father was 30 years old when I made him CEO of Hilderbrand Enterprises. He was green under the collar when he was given this responsibility. Yes, he made numerous mistakes, many poor judgments, and we had some setbacks, but Nathan learned from his mistakes. He had to gain respect not only from within but also from our sister companies. I have watched you mature over the last three years and have full confidence that you can step into your father's shoes. You know the business. You know all the clients, and you have a good rapport with our employees. Yes, you, Andrew, will be the next CEO of Hilderbrand Enterprises."

"Grandfather, there is no way I am ready to take on such responsibility," Andrew replied. "Isn't there someone else in the company more qualified? Perhaps you should assume this role again. You ARE the owner and founder of the company."

"We can discuss this later. Now is not the time. We will

meet after the funeral and discuss this in more detail. We will make some decisions then. For the time being, we need to ask God for His guidance and wisdom."

"I know, CJ. I'm sorry for my angry comment about God, but…" Andrew said.

"I know Andrew, but remember what Scripture tells us: "Be still and know that I am God.[1]" In these difficult times, we need God more than ever.

"Andrew, I have a couple more comments," he went on. "I am 70 years old, and it is time for me to step aside and let a younger, stronger individual carry on the Hilderbrand name. You, Andrew, will be that person. I have complete faith in you, just as I did your father. Oh, I will be a presence for a while to do a bit of coaching and offer some guidance. "However, I will remain in the background while doing so. Trust in God, Andrew, just as your father did. Seek God's guidance and wisdom, and if you do this, you will do just fine."

"Please, give me some time to think about this. Thank you for your support and trust," Andrew replied.

Soon after he and CJ had finished, Andrew's phone rang.

It was Jennie. "Andrew, are you okay? Is there anything I can do?"

"No, I will be alright; it's just going to take some time! I loved them so much, and now they are gone."

"I miss you, Andrew. We haven't visited much since I have gotten back. Let's go have coffee."

"I miss you, too, and coffee would be great."

"I want to catch you up on my parents and their mission work. They phoned me last night with some bad news. We need to finalize a wedding date also."

---

1   New Living Translation, Psalm 46:10

"Yes, we do, and what bad news?"

"Tell you over coffee."

***

Jennie and Andrew arrived at the *In and Out Java Shop*. Before entering, they had a long embrace. They seated themselves, and both ordered lattes, which was their favorite.

"How are your parents? What bad news did you hear last night?"

"As you know, Mom and Dad are serving in Brazil with missionary team members. They were to relocate to Chile. They were planning on being here for our wedding, which now will have to be moved up. However, Dad had a terrible fall and will probably be confined to a leg cast and therapy for at least six months. They don't want us to wait that long but instead asked us to video the wedding, and they could at least watch the video. They insisted on us not waiting. I informed them about your parent's death, and they were heartbroken and will be lifting the Hilderbrand family up in prayer.

"Sorry to hear about your father, and I do so appreciate their prayers."

"Oh, Andrew, I wanted so much to set our wedding date in mid-May, but shouldn't we wait a while longer to give you, CJ, and Sarah time?"

"Yes, I have thought about that and agree. I don't think it would be right to have a Hilderbrand wedding so close to our family funeral."

"How about a mid-June wedding?"

"That's good. I guess I need to look into funeral arrangements."

"That won't be necessary; your grandparents are already

taking care of everything."

"That's too much of a burden for them to do on their own. I need to help, Jennie."

Jennie remarked, "They insisted, and perhaps you should let them do so."

"Yes, you are probably right," answered Andrew. "However, I will call grandfather later this evening and suggest I help with the arrangements. CJ knows everyone in this community. He is a pillar in the church, and I am sure there will be many wanting to be there for him and help with the necessary arrangements."

"I know," remarked Jennie. "CJ did say the church family would be there for all of us. He did, however, say the family members were a different story. I wonder what he meant by that?"

"Well, Jennie, that is a different story. I will explain later, at least attempt to explain the best I can. Now is not the time. It's a long, complicated story."

CHAPTER TWO

The funeral was at Beaumont Calvary Chapel Church Saturday morning, and the church sanctuary was full to capacity. The service concluded with several members giving testimonies describing their relationships with Nathan and Louise. One young woman shared how much she enjoyed the Young Adult Women's Bible study that Louise had led. This study resulted in her acceptance of Jesus as her Lord and Savior.

CJ and Andrew had a difficult time getting through their prepared remembrances. They shared fond memories and how God's mercy touched their lives just by being with Nathan and Louise.

After the service, family and numerous friends made their way to the cemetery. The minister gave his condolences to the family and welcomed everyone. "On behalf of the family, I would like to thank you for being here today to pay our final goodbyes to Nathan and Louise. As an act of remembrance, with reverence and love, we have gathered to place their remains here in this cemetery. We know today that Nathan and Louise are at home with the Heavenly Father in a much better place. Let us now join together in the spirit of prayer and meditation, first by hearing familiar words of Solomon from the book of Ecclesiastes and then a time of silence: 'There is a time for everything: A time to be born; a time to die; a time to plant; a time to harvest; a time to kill; a time to heal; a time to destroy; a time to rebuild; a time to cry; a time to laugh; a time to grieve; a time to dance; a time for scattering stones; a time for gathering stones; a time to hug; a time not to hug; a time to find; a time to lose; a time for keeping; a time for throwing away; a time to tear; a time to repair; a time to be quiet; a time to speak up; a time for loving; a time for hating; a time for war; a time for peace.[2]'"

The Pastor continued. "Now we place these remains in the ground; what has come from the earth goes back to the earth. Now is the time to say your goodbyes by placing flowers on the caskets. We have truly let Nathan and Louise go. Having completed the final task, may we go forth in quiet with a measure of peace so that we may live out our own lives with renewed memory and with deepened love for one another. We have been blessed by life; now go in peace. Amen."

After the service, many friends and church members gathered and offered condolences to the Hilderbrands. They wanted to let the family know they would be there for support whenever they needed it.

---

2   New Living Translation, Ecclesiastes 3:1-8

CHAPTER THREE

$\mathcal{T}$wo months had passed since the funeral of Andrew's parents. Andrew had settled into his role as CEO of Hilderbrand Enterprises and really enjoyed working more closely with the employees. CJ had proven to be a masterful mentor, and Andrew now realized why his father and CJ were so respected in the company.

It was Saturday morning, June 3. Jennie gave Andrew a call. "Hello, Andrew."

"Well, good morning, Jennie. You sound rather chipper this morning."

"Did you have a good jog this morning?"

"Yes, it was a beautiful morning for my jog. However, I must admit that my usual five-mile jogs have become closer to half that. I'm going to have to get up earlier on workdays and build up to that five-mile mark again."

"Andrew, the weather for tomorrow is forecast to be warm and sunny. How about after church we go out to the lake for a picnic?"

"Sounds great."

"I'll make some potato salad and sandwiches."

"That sounds wonderful. I'll pick up the soft drinks."

"See you at church. Love you."

"Love you, too."

"Andrew, please be praying. We have some very important things to discuss and decide on."

"Is something wrong?"

"We'll talk about that tomorrow."

Jennie ended the call, but by the tone of her voice, Andrew was concerned and asked himself some questions. She had not recently mentioned their wedding plans, and lately, she hadn't been her usual bubbly self. *Had something happened to one of her parents? Was she wanting to postpone the wedding? Why didn't she stay for the college commencement ceremonies?* This is one question he had meant to ask earlier, but it had completely slipped his mind. What Andrew would learn in the next 36 hours would certainly answer some of these questions and change both his and Jennie's lives in years to come.

***

After the church service, Andrew and Jennie drove to their favorite spot located just on the outskirts of Beaumont. It was a perfect spot with beautiful shrubs and flowers. In the center of the park was a small lake. Andrew had sensed the tension in Jennie on the way to the park and that tension carried over as they began to eat their lunch. She picked at the potato salad and hadn't touched her sandwich.

"Jennie, something's wrong. Is it your parents? Tell me."

"My parents are fine. It's more than that. Can we walk around the lake?"

Andrew took Jennie's hand, and they began to walk around the lake. To ease the tension, Andrew stopped and skipped some stones across the lake. He had Jennie try the same task, but she wasn't very successful, resulting in some giggles.

After several moments, Jennie became silent as they continued around the lake and suggested they stop at the next park bench.

"Jennie, you're crying; what's wrong?"

"Oh, Andrew, I love you. I can't hide this any longer. I went to see my doctor yesterday after our phone conversation; I know that I am pregnant and …we're pregnant with twins!"

Andrew yelled. "You are what? You're pregnant? How can that be? We were being so very cautious. Do you understand the ramifications of what could happen?"

Jennie answered, "Slow down, Andrew, and yes, I do know what I am saying, and I certainly am aware of the consequences. Don't forget, you are as guilty as I am. We should have known better than this."

"I know, I know, I'm just not sure how to handle this. You know our family background, the squeaky clean, or supposedly squeaky-clean, background."

"What do you mean supposedly squeaky clean?" chided Jennie.

"Remember when I told you I would fill you in on certain family details?" Andrew stated. "I…um…guess this is the time to do so. I have told you that my grandparents have always lived a moral, Christian, religious life. CJ insisted that his will would contain specific clauses. One, that no children out of wedlock would be accepted, and by no means would no one ever be involved with an abortion. Well, my father and mother were quite satisfied with those conditions. I have never seen their will, but I suspect they have the same stipulations and incorporated them into it. That will may have been altered, but I can't say for sure. Did you know my father had an older brother and younger sister?"

Jennie responded, "I had no idea. I always thought he was an only child just as you are."

"I never told you this before," Andrew continued. "My father had a brother who was two years older and a sister who was eight years younger."

"Why didn't you tell me this?" Jennie asked.

"Well, it was something that my parents and grandparents were ashamed of. They didn't talk about it," Andrew explained.

"What happened, Andrew?"

Andrew replied, "My father's older brother, Phillip, and his girlfriend got themselves in the same situation we are now in. She had an abortion, and she and the child did not survive. Phillip tried to hide the whole event, but somehow, my grandparents found out. They were devastated. Phillip knew about the provisions of the will. He did not want to disgrace the family name. He joined the army and fought in the Vietnam War. He was on a dangerous mission with seven other men, and their vehicle struck a mine and all eight men were killed. Of course, my father was also devastated by Phillip's death. They were so close and practically inseparable."

"I'm so sorry. What did your grandparents do?" questioned Jennie.

"They were heartbroken," replied Andrew. "CJ felt like he was responsible for his son's death."

"Because of the will?" Jennie asked.

"I suspect that had a lot to do with it. I think there were a lot of guilty feelings, but neither my parents nor grandparents ever talked about it."

"What about the sister?'

"Very similar circumstances, she got pregnant and left home. About two years later, she wrote a letter telling CJ and Sara how sorry she was for her actions, that she knew she had disgraced the family name and couldn't bear to face them or their friends."

"Wasn't there any forgiveness?" Jennie asked.

"Oh, I'm sure there was. Just the fact that both CJ and Sara are so close to the Lord should have made it easy to forgive Lou Ann and Phillip. Father opened up to me a few years later and told me Sara wrote a letter begging Lou Ann to come home, that she and CJ had forgiven her and loved her very much."

"Did Lou Ann respond?" questioned Jennie.

"We think that she never got the letter."

"Oh no! Why?"

"Nearly two weeks later, Sara and CJ received notification from the authorities in Ohio that they found a suicide notice from Lou Ann. However, Lou Ann was never found," Andrew said, shaking his head.

"I'm so sorry; this had to be heartbreaking for CJ and Sara. They lost two children in a span of three years."

Andrew was silent for a few moments, then responded, "For sure, they lost their son, but the disappearance of Lou Ann remains a mystery. She has never been heard from. It's as if she just disappeared."

"That's awful; they don't even know if she's dead or alive," responded Jennie. "They should never give up hope. Perhaps God is using Lou Ann in a way we could never imagine."

Andrew felt very uncomfortable with the conversation. He walked around the park bench and down to the lake and, after a few minutes, returned to find Jennie praying.

"Jennie, I really miss Dad and Mom. I still can't believe they are gone. I questioned God more than once since the accident and asked for wisdom on how to move forward with our lives."

Jennie was quiet for a few minutes and then went to embrace Andrew. "And now we have to deal with this new dilemma. In James, God tells us to ask for wisdom, and he gives generously, but we must believe and not doubt."

"Thanks, Jennie. I need some quiet time alone with God. Perhaps if we both do some serious soul searching, we can figure this out."

"With God's help, that is," replied Jennie.

"Of course, with God's help," Andrew replied as they embraced. "We will talk more later. It's getting late. We better pack up and head for home. Tomorrow is Monday, and I know CJ has some contracts for him and me to discuss."

CHAPTER FOUR

$\mathcal{T}$he following few days after Jennie's disclosure of her pregnancy were quite stressful for both Jennie and Andrew. Neither knew how they were going to break the news to CJ and Sarah. Jennie spent most of her time in her small apartment, only to go out for occasional walks around the block. She spent many hours in Bible reading and prayer, asking God for forgiveness.

Andrew had a hard time concentrating on his work obligations and did his best to hide his emotions. Fortunately for Andrew, CJ was attending a men's church retreat and was out of the office. CJ would have sensed the tension Andrew was experiencing. During the evening hours, he also spent more time than usual in Bible reading and prayer. He knew Jennie was much more knowledgeable about the Bible, and now he was regretting that he hadn't spent more time in prayer and searching out the scriptures. He knew this had to change in the future.

On Thursday evening, after much deliberation, Jennie gave Andrew a call. "I miss you, Andrew. I've been doing a lot of praying, but so far, God hasn't revealed to me a solution."

"Same here, but one thing is for sure: with my Bible reading and praying, I can certainly sense God's presence, and that is so comforting."

"Oh, Andrew, I'm so glad you shared that. Let's keep praying that the Lord will provide us with an answer."

"CJ called me last night and indicated his retreat was really a blessing but also asked me to visit a good client that was having some minor problems with a product of ours. It sounded simple, but CJ thought it best that I handle it in person. I will be gone for a couple days but will be back by this Sunday. The evenings will give me time for Bible reading and giving our current dilemma a serious thought."

"Drive careful, and I will see you on Sunday. Will miss you!"

***

The out-of-town trip took Andrew longer than anticipated, and he didn't get home until late Saturday night. He had called Jennie to let her know he would be late, but in that call, he sensed a bit of excitement in Jennie's voice.

The church sanctuary was filled Sunday morning, and both Andrew and Jennie felt convicted about even being in church.

However, as the minister got into his message, Jennie took Andrew's hand, and a smile crossed her face. The scripture passage was Romans 8:31-39. Two verses caught Andrew's attention, and the first verse was when Jennie had taken his hand. "Can anything ever separate us from Christ's love? Does it mean He no longer loves us if we have trouble or calamity, or are persecuted, or hungry, or destitute, or in danger, or threatened with death?[3]" Andrew thought to himself that this verse was certainly applicable to Jennie and him.

Jennie squeezed his hand more forcefully when verse 38

---

3   New Living Translation, Romans 8:35

was read. "And I am convinced that nothing can ever separate us from God's love. Neither death nor life, neither angels nor demons, neither our fears for today nor our worries about tomorrow-not even the powers of hell can separate us from God's love.[4]"

After exiting the church, Andrew and Jennie walked to Andrew's car. Jennie gave Andrew a big hug and burst out, "Andrew, can you believe it?"

"What can't you believe?" questioned Andrew.

"I read that exact passage last night. Even though we have committed an awful sin, God still loves us."

"Yes, He does, and He sure works in mysterious ways."

"Have you given any thought to the discussion we had last Sunday? I have tried to come up with a solution on how to not cause CJ and Sara any more grief. Two ideas are possible. One, we can tell them the truth and suffer the consequences," suggested Andrew.

"With the pain, both have suffered, I'm not sure that is feasible. Although it would probably be the best, what is option number two, Andrew?"

Andrew hesitated a few moments. He saw CJ and Sara, who had just come out of the church and were visiting with other church members.

"Abortion."

Jennie was shocked. "What, how could you even suggest such a thing!"

Andrew replied, "I suggested it, but, well, it's not really an option. Forget I even mentioned it."

"No! I can't forget it; is CJ's will really that important to you that you would suggest such a hideous idea, Andrew?" Jennie

---

4   New Living Translation, Romans 8:38

was now in tears. "You even said that the will stipulated absolutely no abortions in the Hilderbrand family."

"I'm so sorry, no, it's not an option. I just do not want to hurt CJ and Sara. I just don't know what to do."

"Andrew, we both have been praying and giving this a lot of thought."

Jennie turned to Andrew and indicated, "I have an idea that just might work. Let's go out to the lake, and I will fill you in on the idea."

After arriving at the lake, the couple got out of the car. Of course, Andrew was excited to hear Jennie's idea. No matter what her idea was, it had to be better than his preposterous abortion plan. Jennie had always thought things out much better than Andrew, and he often thought the Lord was responsible for that. He also knew that her walk with God was much stronger than his. This was something he knew he had to work on, especially now that his mother and father were gone. He had always relied on his father for advice, especially with religious matters. He and his father often sat for hours discussing worldly issues. He remembered his father would always end the discussion with, "Let's see what the Bible says." In every case, God's word always revealed Nathan's understanding of the issue at hand was far superior to his.

"OK, Jennie, let's hear it."

Jennie's reply was, "Not just yet; let's run first and get our blood circulating and hearts pumping," as she took off sprinting and leaving Andrew behind.

"Hold on, not so fast!!"

"Come on, Pokey. I'll beat you to our spot."

"I don't think so." Andrew speeded up but didn't notice the tree root that was in the path. He tripped and fell. Momentarily dazed, he resumed his chase but was unable to catch Jennie and saw her sitting on the bench in a spot surrounded by flowers and shrubs.

"I told you I would beat you to the spot."

"You didn't see me trip and fall, did you?"

"No, I didn't. Are you okay?"

"Yes, but you are faster than I thought you would be. You have been doing some jogging, haven't you?"

"Yes, but now at four months into my pregnancy, I will be quitting my morning jogs."

"Yes, that would be wise. So, what's your idea?" Andrew asked.

"I happened to remember a dear friend I met while in college who now works at an orphanage. I contacted her last night, and, without going into too much detail, I explained the situation. I told her I was carrying twins and was four months pregnant. Maria said there was a very good hospital nearby having a couple of well-qualified pediatricians that have delivered a number of babies that are destined for the orphanage."

Andrew became very quiet and sat there for a moment before answering. "What about the twins, and what would you do while waiting for the delivery?" he questioned.

"I was coming to that. All I have left on my master's is an internship that would take about four or five months. There is a marine biology research lab within a mile of the orphanage."

"How do you know all this, Jennie?"

"I have been doing my homework. Also, I have contacted the research lab, and Dr. Allred, the lab director, has just the project for me. In fact, he is ecstatic that perhaps I would commit. It seems the lab has a project involving starfish that has not drawn much interest from anyone. He asked if I would consider working on such a project, and of course, I jumped at the idea. As you know, I have always been fascinated with small marine critters, including starfish. You can't believe how excited I was when I heard about this project. Is this okay with you, Andrew? Oh, Andrew, we've committed a horrific sin, but God hasn't forgotten us."

"Jennie, you never cease to amaze me, but what about the twins? Where would you live?" questioned Andrew.

"Not to worry, there is a small apartment near the research lab that is available."

"And the twins?" he asked.

Jennie got up and walked around the park bench and placed her hand on Andrew's shoulder, giving him a shoulder massage. "Maria has explained our situation to the orphanage administrator, who evidently had a sister in a similar situation. She understands our dilemma. The orphanage is willing to let Maria care for the twins for the time until we marry. We then would adopt our own sons back."

Andrew stood and took Jennie's hand. There were several couples who were enjoying the park, but Andrew and Jennie did not even notice them. "Well, sounds like you have been busy. I am so sorry for what we are going through. You know, though, we can make this work, Jennie. We will have to cover the fact that they are our own twins."

"Since the orphanage administrator understands our situation, she will certainly know why we want to keep our twins a secret, especially since they will have been born out of wedlock. Of course, we will have to tell CJ and Sara the truth later. The twins won't be the issue. However, their being born out of wedlock will be the difficult part. I remember CJ saying he would like us to fill the house with children after we were married, and twins would be a good start. Oh, Andrew, we can make this work with God's help."

"Yes, I think we can."

As they walked toward their cars, Jennie was reminded of all she had to do in order to get ready to leave. "We better get going. I have a lot to do before leaving." They both started walking back. When they arrived at the car, Andrew hugged Jennie, and they held the embrace for several moments.

"I have a meeting with CJ tomorrow morning at the corporate office. I will fill him in on your project in Baja. Oh my, CJ is calling me now." Andrew took the call.

"Can you come to my office? I want to go over the Bergstrom contract with you. It won't take very long since most of the details have been finalized, thanks to you."

Andrew replied, "Be there at 8 a.m. tomorrow morning."

"That would be fine. See you then."

***

The next morning, Andrew found CJ at his desk shuffling through a pile of papers. "Morning, Andrew. Did you have a good weekend?"

"Yes, I spent some time with Jennie. She will be leaving in a few days for the UCSD Marine Lab in Baja. She will be gone for five to six months to do an internship to earn her masters' degree."

With a surprised look on his face, CJ commented, "That long? I had no idea. Where will she stay?"

"She has found an apartment near the research lab where she will do her intern work," Andrew explained.

"That woman is a trooper. You've found a good one, Andrew."

"Yes, I have."

"Tying the knot when she gets done?"

"Yes, we are and will be moving into Mom and Dad's house."

CJ nodded his head. "Good, good, and having kids."

Andrew looked at the pictures of his father, CJ, and himself in their baseball uniforms on the wall behind CJ's desk. "Yes, having kids," replied Andrew with a sly look on his face, staring out the window.

"Not to change the subject, Andrew, but we better go over those contracts. We have a lot to decide on."

CHAPTER FIVE

*J*enny had so much to do to prepare for her move. Everything was happening so fast after talking to Andrew. She had done a lot to prepare mentally, but a thousand things remained physically before she could leave. She had many phone calls to make. First, she called the research lab to establish a timeline for her project.

A gentleman's voice answered the phone, "Hello, Tidewater Research Center, Dr. Allred speaking."

"This is Jennie Summers."

"Oh, Jennie, how are you?"

"Fine, thank you," Jennie responded. "We visited last week. I'm calling to find out when I could start my intern project?"

Laughing, Dr. Allred answered, "Tomorrow, if you would like."

"I have a few things to finish up here to get ready. Would next Monday be alright?" Jennie replied.

"That would be fine. I'm looking forward to having you on board. I think you will find the project challenging and rewarding. My office is in the left-wing of the lab, room number twenty-five."

"Thanks. I'm looking forward to the project. See you next Monday." The quick response of the lab director caught Jennie completely off guard. She had not expected to be leaving this soon. Next Monday would only give her five days to get all the necessary arrangements and all the packing completed. Jennie wondered if she could do it.

After Jennie hung up the phone, she started running around her apartment, picking through the closets and drawers. She threw some of her clothes on the couch and finally sat down on her big chair in the living room. Next to her chair was her Bible, and she began looking for a certain passage that she had remembered. *But the Lord our God is merciful and forgiving, even though we have rebelled against him.*[5] She bowed her head in prayer and thanked God for giving her that verse.

Jennie needed to talk to Andrew.

Andrew answered her call., "Hi, babe. What's up?"

"I just spoke with the research lab director, and I will be leaving on Monday morning."

"Are you kidding me? That soon? That is only five days from now."

"Oh, Andrew, I just feel terrible about this. Are we doing the right thing?"

"I have asked myself that question many times. I have prayed, but God hasn't been clear with an answer. I know God forgives us, but just not sure CJ will, and I just don't think I want to take that risk just yet."

"Yes, Andrew, I agree. You're right. I love CJ and Sara, and telling them now may be too much for them since you are the only hope they have."

"No, they always have the Lord, Jennie."

---

5   New Living Translation, Daniel 9:9

"And Andrew, so do we."

"Can I help you get ready?"

"No, there's really not much you can do. I have a few woman things to take care of. Perhaps a nice dinner Sunday evening at our favorite spot."

"You're on!"

Jennie added, "By the way, how was your meeting with CJ?"

"Fine, CJ adores you and is so anxious for us to, as he said, 'Tie the knot and fill the house with kids.'" Jennie and Andrew both giggled. "And you know, Jennie, that may start happening sooner than anticipated."

The next three days went by much too quickly, but Jennie was able to get everything packed and all the details organized. She purchased a couple sets of maternity outfits she would be needing. Not to raise any red flags, she had purchased these items from a women's apparel store in a nearby town. Fortunately, she had notified her landlord several weeks earlier, and now she was glad that she had been preparing for her future marriage and given most of her belongings to a local church thrift store. She knew that after their marriage, they would be moving to Andrew's parents' home, and she wouldn't need any items but personal belongings.

Sunday morning at church, Jennie and Andrew joined CJ and Sara in their usual pew. The pastor opened in prayer, and then the worship leader announced that several of the parishioners had requested a number of old hymns, asked all to rise, and continued, "You all know these oldies, so I expect these walls to shake this morning." With that, the pianist started playing the first hymn, which just happened to be 'What a Friend We Have in Jesus.' Both Sara and CJ had angelic voices, and their harmonizing was beautiful. Halfway through the first stanza, Jennie started crying, and she reached over and squeezed Andrew's hand. Halfway through 'Softly and Tenderly,' Jennie could no longer hold back her tears and quickly left the sanctuary. Andrew, also with red eyes, knew exactly why Jennie left the service. After a couple more hymns, Jennie returned and seemed to have regained her composure. Andrew took her hand as they listened to the sermon.

After the service, the Hilderbrands all gathered outside the church, and after many hugs and tears, they said their good-byes to Jennie.

After leaving the church, Jennie went to her apartment to double-check and satisfy herself that she was all set for her departure the next morning. She had dressed for their dinner date and opened her Bible to the book of Psalms. The Psalms were her favorite book of the Bible, and she had memorized many of the passages. Her eyes became misty as she read, "Have mercy on me, O God, because of your unfailing love. Because of your great compassion, blot the stain of my sins. Wash clean from my guilt. Purify me from my sin. For I recognize my rebellion; it haunts me day and night.[6]"

She was startled when Andrew called. "Are you okay?"

"Oh, Andrew, I'm sorry. I was in the Psalms and lost track of time. I will be there in fifteen minutes."

As she walked into the restaurant, she waved at Andrew sitting at their corner table. Soft candlelight, music, and a vase of roses on their table created a romantic atmosphere.

Andrew waved and stood to greet her. Andrew, wearing dress slacks, a sports coat, and a white shirt, whistled softly as he hugged Jennie and kissed her cheek.

"Wow, you are so beautiful; you're especially pretty in that

---

6   New Living Translation, Psalms 51:1,2,3

ocean blue gown."

Laughing, she twirled and said, "Well, you look rather dapper yourself, Andrew."

"You are gorgeous; I'm a lucky man," stated Andrew.

The waiter came over to hand them a menu, but Andrew told him that a menu was not necessary. "We will both have the prime rib, medium rare, salads and a baked potato, and waters with a wedge of lemon."

"That was perfect, Andrew; you nailed it."

"What time will you be leaving tomorrow, Jennie?"

"Around sixish, it's about a seven-hour drive. I'm going to miss you so much the next few months."

"Yes, me too. I will get down as often as I can, but I know CJ has some major assignments and contracts he wants completed before winter. Some of those contracts will mean out-of-state travel. I just want to make sure I'm not out of state when the delivery time draws near."

Andrew and Jennie enjoyed their meal, the beauty of the restaurant, and the closeness of each other. Andrew asked, "Want to share a dessert?"

"No thanks, I'm good."

Jennie looked away. Then with tears, she said, "Oh, Andrew, I'm scared. What if the twins aren't normal or there is a medical problem? We know nothing about the doctors."

"Didn't your friend Maria say there were good doctors in the nearby hospital?" questioned Andrew.

"Yes, she did, but I feel like I am going against God's will."

"We don't always know what God's will is. I have questioned God's will in my life many times since Mom and Dad were killed. Was that God's will, Jennie?"

"I don't know. I can't answer that. I had better go. I have a number of last-minute items to take care of before leaving in the morning."

Andrew grabbed the check and went to pay at the register. After leaving the restaurant, they approached their vehicles and embraced and hugged for several moments.

"Good night, Andrew. I will call you along the way and when I get to Baja."

"Please do, and drive carefully." Andrew paused for a moment. "And Jennie, I will be praying for us. This will work out. Just a few more months and we will be Mr. and Mrs. Hilderbrand in our own home with kids needing diapers changed."

"I can hardly wait. It's been a wonderful evening, Andrew."

At her apartment, Jennie loaded her belongings into her car, readying everything to leave the next morning.

CHAPTER SIX

$\mathscr{B}$y 6 a.m., Jennie was driving the scenic route along the coast, enjoying the beautiful scenery. This route would mean more driving time, but Jennie had always enjoyed this drive. She loved the ocean with its pounding waves – the whole seascape. She spotted whales spouting on a few occasions; the ocean fascinated her. Just walking around the tidepools and viewing all the little sea creatures had always been one of her favorite activities as a child when her family vacationed in Oregon. Her interest in these little sea specimens motivated her to pursue Marine Biology, but she knew that such a career could be put on hold after marrying Andrew, especially with the twins' a part of their family.

Jennie knew her current circumstance could possibly create some difficult relationships within the family but was so thankful for Andrew's accepting the announcement of her pregnancy. She had known nothing about the family will until recently with Andrew's disclosing the terms. She could only hope and pray that CJ and Sara would be forgiving. After Andrew's disclosure of what occurred with two children and the loss of Andrew's father, the forgiving part might be difficult, maybe impossible. But she was so thankful for CJ and Sara's strong relationship with the Lord.

As she was traveling, she enjoyed Christian radio with its wonderful music. Singing along with the music, lost in her own thoughts, it was almost 9 a.m. when Jennie just happened to look down at the gas gauge and saw that she was almost out of gas. Luckily, she spotted a gas station and had her tank filled. She handed the attendant her card to pay for the gas. When he had returned, he commented to her that he liked her music and that many customers stop for gas but not very often does he hear Christian music playing. Jennie smiled and waved to the attendant and continued her drive to Baja.

By 1 p.m., she was in Baja. She found her apartment and was pleased with its location. The ocean view from the large bay window in the living room was gorgeous. The small apartment was compact and spotlessly clean. The bed was comfortable, and she felt almost at home.

Jennie called Andrew. He answered, "Hi, Babe. How was the drive?"

"Fine, Oh Andrew, it was beautiful! I took the scenic route and just got here a while ago. I love the ocean, God's majesty in action, don't you think?"

"God has created many wonders, and the ocean is certainly one of them. How's the apartment?" Andrew was curious. "Are you going to be ok there? How's the bed?"

"It's comfortable, and I'll have some fun putting things in order. Now I'm hitting the shower and then to bed. I am exhausted."

"I bet you are. Get some sleep. Oh, by the way, love you."

"Love you too. Good night."

Before bedtime, Jennie called Maria. "Hello Maria, this is

Jennie, and I arrived just moments ago."

"How was the trip?"

"Great, I took the scenic ocean route, and it was beautiful."

"I'm so excited and can't wait to see you again."

"I will visit the lab first thing in the morning but should have time in the afternoon for a woman-to-woman visit."

"Sounds great. See you tomorrow afternoon."

Maria and Jennie had spoken many times, but Maria had never told Jennie about her failed marriage and, under the circumstances, would not unless Jennie asked her. Tomorrow's reunion would just be a time of giggles and woman talk.

The next morning, Dorothy, the receptionist, met Jennie at the front desk of the lab. "May I help you?"

"Yes, I am Jennie Summers."

"Oh yes, Miss Summers. Mr. Allred said I should be expecting you this morning. I will let him know you are here."

Mr. Allred came through the door with a big smile. "Good morning, Jennie; pleased to meet you."

"Likewise."

"Dorothy, Jennie will be with us for five or six months doing her internship. She will be working in the aquarium complex doing some work with starfish. She will need a password code for lab entrance. Could you please take care of that?"

"Yes, right away."

Mr. Allred took Jennie to show her around the facility where she would be working.

"How is the apartment? Will it work out okay for you?"

"Yes, it is quite comfortable and has a beautiful view of the ocean. Also, it will be a nice walk to and from the lab."

They entered the lab area, where Mr. Allred entered a code to enter the aquarium complex. Jennie watched several lab workers busy with projects. As Jennie followed him into the aquarium, she couldn't help but notice that most of the interns were young ladies except for three older men. All the workers smiled and gave her a warm welcome. Jennie wondered to herself just how friendly these cohorts would be when she really started showing her pregnancy. But she would cross that bridge when she came to it.

"This is where you will be spending most of your time. We have a number of interns, and you will find them to be most helpful." Mr. Allred continued showing Jennie around the lab, and then they exited the aquarium and went back into his office to discuss details of Jennie's project.

For the next four months, Jennie practically worked nonstop on her assigned project. To her surprise, she liked her lab coworkers. They were friendly and helpful and didn't bother her when her pregnancy became obvious. God had certainly answered her anxious and ongoing prayers.

Andrew had only visited Jennie three times since the start of her internship. Their dedication to their workloads made travel to see each other difficult. Andrew was excited to see Jennie, now in her eighth month of pregnancy, and decided on the spur of the moment to surprise her with a visit. Today was Saturday, and he hoped she would be at her apartment. Upon his arrival, he parked out of sight, went to the front door, and knocked.

"Just a minute, be right there."

Andrew remained silent. He really wanted to surprise her. Jennie opened the door.

"Oh wow, Andrew, what a surprise!" She leaped into Andrew's arms and cried tears of joy. "You are a stinker. I'm so happy you came but look at me. I'm as big as an elephant."

Andrew replied, "But you're still gorgeous. Are you okay? How's the project going?"

"It's going well. Mr. Allred and my coworkers have been wonderful to work with."

"Yes, but are you okay?"

"Considering all things, I'm feeling like an eighth-month pregnant woman. I'm a lot more tired than usual. I'm so glad my project is near completion because lately I have been forgetting little things, and it has really bugged me."

"Is that normal? Have you spoken with your doctor about these symptoms?"

"Yes, and he said these are normal and to be expected. He was pleased with how I'm doing. Andrew, is everything okay at work? Have you missed me?"

"You know I have. I've had a few business trips, but other than that, everything is fine at Hilderbrand Enterprises."

"How are CJ and Sara?"

"They are fine, and both ask about you all the time."

"Andrew, I pray for them a lot and how they will respond to us when we show up with twins after getting back home."

"I want us to be married before that happens."

"How can we make that work?"

Andrew was silent for several moments and then asked, "How close is your relationship with Maria?"

"We are very close and were nearly inseparable in college. Why do you ask?"

"I have given this much thought and a lot of prayer. I have a proposal to think about and talk over with Maria. After the twins are born, we could have Maria care for them for a few days. During that time, we would get married and return for the twins. Of course, it would mean separation from the babies and probably a simple marriage, but if Maria is willing, I think we could make it work. What do you think?"

"Oh, Andrew, I just don't know. A simple wedding is fine, but I sure hate the thought of being separated from our babies. It would be for only a short time, wouldn't it?"

"Yes, very short."

"I will visit with Maria this week, but I'm sure it will be okay with her."

"Good."

"Andrew, who would have thought our big mistake eight months ago would have created so many difficulties?"

"Perhaps God."

"Yes, for sure God. I will be so glad when this is all behind us, and we can start out as a God-fearing family."

CHAPTER SEVEN

*J*ennie completed her lab work and was satisfied that her project had gone well. She also knew her delivery time was close at hand. On the evening of November 1, after nightly Bible reading, Jennie had the inclination to visit Maria. "Is God speaking to me? Maybe this is the time." On several occasions, Jennie had walked to Maria's apartment, but on this chilly November evening, she drove. She arrived at Maria's apartment and was greeted.

"Thanks, Maria; I hope I didn't catch you at a bad time."

"No, not at all; I was just doing some reading."

"Maria, I can't thank you enough for what you are doing for me. How can I ever repay you?"

Maria responded, "No need to repay, just have healthy boys." Maria gave Jennie a big hug with a smile.

"You did say that the doctor next door to the orphanage is a good one? He has always seemed so in my previous visits. He has spoken very highly of you, Maria."

"Yes, he is very good and has delivered many healthy babies. As you know, he is only a short distance from here, which is very convenient. Because of the short distance involved, the clinic has even requested my assistance on a few occasions. By the way, is Andrew going to be here when your time comes?"

"We have discussed that, and both of us have decided it might be best if he wasn't here. Not knowing the exact time, and Andrew is quite busy with some very important contracts. He will come to see the boys after their birth. He wanted so much to be present, but, well, you know, we want to keep this under the radar."

Maria exclaimed, "I understand."

"Maria, did you ever think about marriage and raising a family?"

Maria looked away and seemed very reluctant to answer. "I was married, but it didn't work out."

Jennie commented, "I'm so sorry. Don't you miss not having a family?"

"I miss it very much, and that's the reason our marriage didn't work out. We both wanted children, but I couldn't get pregnant, and he didn't want to adopt. He took it very hard and finally asked for a divorce. I loved children so much, and the orphanage was the next best thing, and this is where I ended up."

At that point, Jennie grabbed her stomach and started shaking and gasping.

With panic in her voice, Maria asked, "Jennie, are you okay?"

"I think it's time!"

"I'll call the clinic. You sit still."

"Hurry, Maria."

Maria went to call the clinic while Jennie sat nervously on the couch. Maria returned and helped Jennie walk to her car. She helped Jennie get seated in the car, and away they went to the clinic.

"Hang in there, Jennie; we will be there in two minutes!"

"I am going to make it. Just please hurry!"

They were at the clinic in good time and were met by a couple of aides. The aides rushed her into the doctor's office. From there, she was rushed into the delivery room with the aid of the doctor. Maria followed along as far as she could go.

"Nurse! Prepare for delivery," the doctor commanded. "This young lady is about ready to deliver." Maria was ushered to the waiting room, where she continued to pace as she waited. While she waited, she tried to make a call to Andrew on her cell phone, but the phone reception kept cutting out. Finally, the call went through.

"Hello," Andrew answered.

In Spanish, Maria responded, "This is Maria. Jennie wanted me to call you. She just went into the delivery room. She is having a baby, I mean babies."

"Maria, slow down. You are speaking in Spanish, and I don't understand a word you are saying," replied Andrew.

"I'm sorry, Jennie is having a baby, I mean babies," she said, speaking in English. "I think anytime now."

From the delivery room, she could hear a baby crying.

Maria held her phone up so that Andrew could hear. "Do you hear the baby?"

"Yes, I hear the baby."

Andrew, in his apartment, jumped up and down, gave a thumbs up, and started pacing around his apartment. No doubt Andrew was excited with the news and the sound of a crying baby. He then could hear a second baby crying.

"Now can you hear two babies?"

"Yes, Maria, I can. Tell Jennie I will be there tomorrow."

"I will. Jennie will be so excited for you to come, and I will get to meet you."

"Yes, Andrew replied, "that will be good. This is so exciting. I can't believe I'm a daddy."

"I better go now. Later, I will let Jennie know you will be here tomorrow."

"Thanks, Maria."

Andrew was ecstatic. After closing out the call, he danced around his apartment, hardly able to contain himself. After thinking about it, he picked up his phone and dialed CJ.

"CJ, I would like to ask a favor of you."

"Go ahead," CJ replied.

"I know it is really short notice, but I would like to make a trip to Baja tomorrow and surprise Jennie."

CJ answered, "By all means. You deserve some relaxation. You have put in some long hours the last several weeks. Stay a few days and give my regards to Jennie and let her know Sara and I miss her."

"Thanks, I will."

***

The next morning Andrew headed to Baja via the shortest route. He drove right to the clinic and was met in the waiting area by a Hispanic woman.

"You must be Andrew," said the woman.

"And you must be Maria. I'm pleased to meet you, and thank you so much for accommodating Jennie."

"It has been my pleasure. We have caught up with a lot of 'woman' talk. Jennie has filled me in on your circumstances, and I think you two are doing the right thing. Follow me; Jennie is so thrilled you came down and can't wait for you to see the twins."

"I can't wait," exclaimed Andrew.

Maria led Andrew down a short hallway and stopped and tapped on the closed door. "I will leave you two alone now," remarked Maria.

Andrew heard Jennie say come in. He opened the door and entered Jennie's room. Jennie was lying on the bed with the twins in a small crib beside her. Both twins were asleep.

"Oh, Andrew, I am so glad you came. You must be tired after the drive."

Andrew walked over to Jennie, kissed her, and then went over to see the twins.

"Seeing you and the twins, I forgot about being tired. Are you ok? Are the boys alright?" Andrew asked.

"Yes, yes, I am fine, and the twins have been great. All they have done is sleep and you know what else little babies do."

"I wish I could have been here for the delivery. Did everything go ok? Was the doctor good?" Andrew questioned.

"The doctor was great, and I want you to meet him tomorrow. Andrew, when the twins wake up, I want you to see something they both have. It's actually quite a coincidence, and it's just amazing how the Lord works, perhaps His sense of humor, but I've never seen anything like it."

With a look of concern, Andrew asked, "What is it? Is something wrong?"

Both twins woke up and began fussing. Andrew was shown the birthmarks on both boys that were under the armpits. Although small, they were quite obvious.

"That is incredible; I had a birthmark in the same area when I was born. My folks had it removed when I was about three years old. It was a simple procedure. At least that is what they told me," Andrew explained.

"Yes, that's what the doctor told me also. He called the marks wine something."

Andrew was all smiles and then broke into laughter. Jennie started laughing also.

"Oh, Andrew, I know I'm terrible with medical terms."

Andrew answered, "I have seen the marks before, and I suspect they are port wine marks."

"Yes, that's what he called them," replied Jennie.

Andrew explained, "They can be removed with some simple laser therapy."

Andrew looked in the bassinet and had a big smile on his face. Jennie took Andrew's hand as she looked at the twins.

"My, oh my," Andrew exclaimed, "those are two sharp-looking boys!"

"They are adorable, aren't they," Jennie added. "Mick and Jake."

"I like them, and just how did you decide on those names?"

"Actually, Maria helped me. I was going to call you and get your input, but Mick and Jake just popped out. I know the way you, your father, and CJ loved baseball, and they just sounded like good ballplayer names."

CJ and Andrew's father had all played professional ball. And in fact, baseball had been a passion for all three men. Not only had they all played on the diamond, but all three had also been pitchers. As the player tales had gone and been shared over time, all three were good at their positions.

Andrew had prayed for a son with whom he could share his baseball knowledge and skills, and now perhaps that prayer would be answered with not only a son but two sons. Of course, that would be a little way off.

"They certainly do have a baseball ring to them."

Both twins began to cry, becoming a bit more restless and moving around in their crib.

"There, Andrew, you can see the birthmarks better now."

"I see them, and they shouldn't be a problem." Andrew stood up, yawning. He walked over and took Jennie's hand, and they both watched the twins for a while.

"It's getting very late, and maybe I should get some rest. You need to rest, too," said Andrew. "We have a lot to talk about tomorrow. It's really nice of Maria to let me stay in her house tonight."

"Yes, Maria is a wonderful woman, and she is on duty tonight at the orphanage. She lives right next door. Sleep in if you can."

"Are you kidding," remarked Andrew. "I will probably be here before you wake up. This is so exciting!"

After kissing her on the forehead, he started towards the door and then turned back to Jennie. "You wanted me to meet the doctor. I almost forgot."

"Yes, he will be here early in the morning. Perhaps you can see him when you come in," replied Jennie.

"Good idea. Good night, Jennie."

The next morning Andrew left the house and walked down the path to the orphanage clinic. He stopped and observed the directions to the clinic's physician and arrived at the office door. He knocked at the door, and the doctor opened the door. "Come in and have a seat."

Andrew entered the office and took a seat opposite the doctor's desk.

"I presume you are the father of the twins," stated the doctor.

"Yes, yes I am."

"I am Doctor Roberts."

"I am Andrew Hilderbrand."

"Yes, Jennie told me you would be coming," replied the doctor.

"Andrew, you are a very lucky man. Jennie is a wonderful lady and, yes, she did give me a few details about your situation. Here at the clinic, we get all kinds of situations, but we have never had one quite like yours and Jennie's. What we hear here stays here. You and Jennie can rest assured of that."

Andrew replied, "Thank you, Doctor Roberts. That is very comforting to hear."

Doctor Roberts stood up and began walking around the office and then sat down behind his desk with a look of concern on his face. "Andrew, there is something I have to tell you. I have not told Jennie. I wanted to tell you first, and it might be best you share with Jennie, or we both can."

Andrew became very nervous, not knowing what to expect. "What is it, Doc? Is she ok? Are the twins alright? They have birthmarks. I had one myself."

"The birthmarks are not a problem, Andrew. They can easily be removed in two or three years. However, there were some complications during delivery. Jennie and the twins will be fine."

"What is it then, Doc?"

"Because Jennie delivered twins, her birth canal may have suffered some damage. If so, she may not be able to deliver a child in the future. I am not saying this is out of the question, but it is certainly a possibility. The damage may heal, but I just wanted you to know. I've seen a number of these situations where twins and even triplets were anticipated, and the mother had no complications with subsequent deliveries."

"Thanks for sharing this with me first. I know more children are in our plans for the future, and Jennie will be devastated to know that natural birth may not be an option."

The doctor replied, "I know Jennie has a strong relationship with the Lord, and from what I hear, you have a good relationship also. At this point, you two will just have to pray that God's will be done."

"Yes, that's all we can do. Doctor Roberts, I would like for us both to share this with Jennie. Are you available to do it now? This may be quite difficult for Jennie to accept, so let's go together."

"Yes, let's visit Jennie now," added Doctor Roberts.

Andrew and Doctor Roberts both stood and left the office. They walked down the hall to Jennie's room. Andrew knocked on the door, and they heard Jennie say, "Come on in." They entered the room.

"Well, this is a surprise."

"How are you and the boys doing, Jennie?" Andrew asked. Jennie looked a bit puzzled and looked from Andrew to Doctor Roberts.

"We are fine. Is there something wrong?"

"Jennie, Dr. Roberts just explained to me some concerns he had that may create some issues in the future with having children," stated Andrew. "He thought it best to share with me before discussing with you."

Dr. Roberts took a seat across from Jennie, who was sitting on the bed with the twins lying beside her. He cleared his throat and slowly went into detail, explaining Jennie's situation. He left nothing out but made his explanation easy for the layman to understand. "I'm sorry, Jennie, to have to share this expecting you will want more children. As I told Andrew, I have seen these complications before, and additional children were successfully delivered."

"Dr. Roberts, it's not news I wanted to hear, but thank you for sharing with Andrew and me."

To Andrew's surprise, Jennie took Dr. Robert's explanation of her situation much better than expected. Her only comment and one that both Andrew and Dr. Roberts would probably never forget, was, "If it's God's will for more children or not, may His will be done." Andrew knew that Jennie had been struggling with her pregnancy. What he and Jennie had done was not something that believers and part of God's family should have ever done to begin with, but that was in the past, and now it was time to move forward with their lives. She had come to accept whatever plans God had in store for them. Neither Andrew nor Jennie had any idea how those plans of acceptance would play out in the years to come.

After a good night's rest, Jennie, Andrew, and Maria were relaxing in Maria's living room. The twins were asleep in their bassinet. The three were discussing actions they would be taking for the next few days.

Jennie commented to Maria, "We are so excited that you are willing to care for the boys at the orphanage for a few days."

"I have several days of vacation time, and I would love the opportunity to care for the boys," responded Maria.

"How can we ever repay you, Maria?" asked Andrew. "Jennie and I will have our wedding as soon as we return home. In fact, I have thought about calling CJ to let him know we are getting married here. After all, he and Sara got married by a justice of the peace. CJ told me in secret he and Sara really didn't like big formal weddings."

"In light of the circumstances," Jennie added, "we should have a church wedding but nothing lavish. It would really send up a red flag if we married here and then showed up with twins. Our church family would be so disappointed if we didn't get married in our church, especially since the Hildebrands have been so instrumental in not only the church but the community as well."

"Regardless of what our church family thinks, we will get our sons into our lives very soon. Sooner or later, we will have to share with friends and family what has happened and suffer the consequences," replied Andrew.

Jennie's wheels were turning as she responded, "I think we just have to pray and let God take control. He certainly knows what's best for us."

"Hmm," Andrew questioned for a moment, "Yes, you are right. I think our next big decision is how long we leave the twins under Maria's care before returning to formally adopt."

"Oh, Andrew, I want it to be a short time," chided Jennie. "CJ and Sara are anxious for us to get married. I doubt they would object to a spur-of-the-moment wedding."

"The shorter, the better," commented Andrew. "It may take a while to get everything taken care of back home. Is that ok with you, Maria?"

"Certainly, take as long as you need," Maria responded. "I will look after those boys as if they were my own. The boys can be in the orphanage with me."

"Oh, Maria, you are such an angel, and may God truly bless you. We want you to call us every day to let us know how the twins and you are doing," replied Jennie.

"I will, and I can also send a letter if necessary. Should there be any problems with the phone system, there is a postal drop a couple blocks down the street. I only tell you this because there have been a few occasions in which the phones did not work, and cell reception has been terrible. I just pray this won't be the case."

Andrew looked at Jennie and walked around Maria's apartment, gazing out the window for a while, and then turned to Jennie and Maria. He was a bit concerned about the phone problems Maria mentioned. "How frequent are these phone problems, Maria?"

Maria answered, "Only when we have severe storms, which by the way, are unpredictable in our area. I believe we were out of phone service and power three times last year. The most severe storm shut down phone and power service for three days."

"Oh my," Jennie commented. "We certainly hope that doesn't happen this year."

"Well, Jennie, we had better enjoy these boys the rest of the day. I informed CJ and Sara we would be returning home tomorrow and we had a wedding to arrange."

Maria commented, "You two must be excited."

"Yes, we are, and finally," Jennie stated as she looked at Maria and winked.

All three enjoyed fussing around with the twins, watching their every movement, and enjoying their little facial expressions. Jennie and Andrew took turns trading them with each other and cuddling them.

"I'm going to miss these little guys so much," Jennie commented. "Maria, please call us every day."

"I will. You can be sure of that."

Andrew spoke up, "Well, Jennie, it's time for us to say goodbye to our family, at least for a few days."

"Yes, I know," Jennie stated hesitantly.

Jennie and Andrew got ready to leave, laid the twins in

their bassinet, and both gave Maria a big hug. Jennie leaned down to give each of the boys a final kiss before they left the house to get in their cars for the long drive home.

They each took the scenic route, seeing the beauty of God's majesty that Andrew had missed on his way down. The drive along the California coast was always a relaxing and scenic drive this time of year. With the numerous turnouts, it wasn't difficult to pull out and observe both blue and humpback whales on their migration journey to the waters off the coast of Mexico and then on their return trip back to Alaska. Before their trip, Jennie and Andrew had arranged to rendezvous at one such pullout to enjoy the scenic ocean view and hopefully spot some whales. Their stop was well rewarded with large ocean waves, blue sky, numerous shorebirds, and several surfacing and spouting whales. It was a difficult site to leave, but they decided it best to continue their trip homeward.

As Jennie drove, she prayed. "Father in heaven, I thank you so much for two healthy boys. I pray for your watch care over the twins and Maria. I pray that you would forgive me and Andrew for the sin we have committed. What we did was wrong. We should have known better. I pray that you would give us wisdom in helping us through this situation and help us to communicate to CJ, Sara, and others as we conduct our lives and care for these boys. Help them understand and still have loving hearts. I pray especially for the relationship between CJ and Andrew. I pray for understanding and forgiveness between them. Jesus, I thank you and give you the praise. Amen."

After praying, Jennie had a look of contentment and a slight smile on her face. After the long trip back home, Jennie and Andrew arrived at Jennie's apartment. Jennie had contacted her previous landlord and arranged to stay in a small side apartment for a few days after returning home from Baja. After unpacking, they went to Jennie's apartment porch and relaxed in her sofa swing. "Andrew, I just pray this will work out OK."

"I agree," commented Andrew. "Jennie, they are beautiful boys."

"Yes, they are, and I already miss them."

Before Andrew left for home, he told Jennie that tomorrow, Saturday, he would drop by and pick her up, and they would go and visit with CJ and Sara. He would let them know that they would be stopping by. Jennie's reply was, "Give me a buzz when you are ready."

"Will do; see you in the morning."

The next morning, Andrew arrived at Jennie's, and on their way to the elder Hilderbrands, they discussed a few small details they wanted to share about the upcoming wedding. They specifically wanted to make it clear they wanted a simple wedding.

"Good morning, you two," welcomed Sara. "Come in; it's so good to see both of you. It has been a while. CJ and I are so excited you are finally going to get married. CJ will join us in a bit. I think he is about finished with his call." They all proceeded to the living room and were about to take seats as CJ arrived and greeted them.

"Jennie, it's good to see you. It's been a few months."

"Yes, it has," stated Jennie, "And it's good to be home."

"How did your project go?" inquired CJ.

"It went very well. I finished the project, and I should receive my Master's degree soon. I may have to go back to take care of some loose ends at the lab."

"The Lord has been good to you."

Jennie glanced at Andrew with a bit of concern and then

responded to CJ. "Yes, He has. In fact, the Lord truly got me through this."

"I understand you two have finally decided to tie the knot?" questioned CJ.

Andrew replied, "Yes, we have, and that's the reason for meeting with you and Sara this morning. I know Mom and Dad had a very small wedding, and I believe you and Sara have indicated big formal and elaborate weddings are not your cup of tea either. Would you two be disappointed if Jennie and I just had a small ceremony as well?"

Jennie responded, "I thought I wanted a big church wedding, but after discussing with Andrew, we both prefer a small wedding ceremony. My biggest concern was how our church congregation would respond."

"You two leave that to Sara and I. We will handle the church family. Won't we, Sara?"

"We certainly will, and there will be no questions asked. This wedding will work out just fine. Don't you worry."

Andrew and Jennie were pleased that the grandparents were so willing to deal with the church members. Neither could hold back their smiles because of how CJ and Sara responded.

"Problem solved," stated Andrew.

CJ and Sara quickly went behind the scenes and started making arrangements. Without letting the young couple know, they contacted everybody they could get ahold of in the church to inform them about the wedding but to keep it confidential to surprise Andrew and Jennie since they had requested a small, simple ceremony.

The response by the church members was overwhelming.

A week later, the wedding took place in their home church. The church was packed, much to the surprise of Jennie and

Andrew. CJ and Sara had obviously been very busy behind the scenes. This was not a lavish wedding with all the pomp and circumstance that normally accompany a church wedding. It was a simple wedding with Andrew's close friend of many years serving as the best man while Jennie's best friend served as maid of honor.

Because of the circumstances, a honeymoon by the newlyweds was put on hold. The next three days after the wedding was spent moving from apartments to the home inherited by Andrew. The couple could not wait to move into the large comfortable house and get settled with their two sons. Jennie had informed both CJ and Sara that she would have to return to Baja to tidy some loose ends, and she and Andrew had discussed at great length how they were going to handle those loose ends. They had both been in a lot of prayer on exactly how they were going to do so. Little did either know how the Lord would be moving in their lives the next few years.

As promised, Maria had phoned Jennie every day since their return home, including the evening of the wedding. She informed Jennie and Andrew that the twins were doing great and were beautiful little boys. Of course, these updates on the twins only made the newlyweds more anxious to be together as a family in their own home. However, two days had passed with no word from Maria, and the young parents were becoming very concerned.

"Andrew, I am getting worried. We haven't heard from Maria in two days, no calls, no letters, nothing. When I try Maria's phone, there is nothing. I have tried the orphanage phone and no response. In fact, there isn't even a ring on the other end."

"You sure you have the right numbers?" Andrew asked.

"Positive!!"

Andrew's comment was, "I think we had better take a trip in the morning."

"To the orphanage?" Jennie asked.

"Yes, to the orphanage. I will let CJ know we will be gone for a couple days."

Andrew gave no reason for the sudden trip, and of course, CJ assumed the trip was a mini-honeymoon getaway. Andrew went along with CJ's assumption.

CHAPTER EIGHT

The next morning Andrew and Jennie left the house with only a small overnight bag. They were both very quiet as they drove to the orphanage. When they arrived, Jennie started sobbing. They both exited the car and ran to the charred remains of the orphanage.

"Dear God," stated Jennie, "no, this cannot be, please Father, this didn't happen."

Andrew went to Jennie and wrapped his arms around her. They both started walking through the burned-out remains and Maria's attached apartment.

"Dear God, this can't be, first my parents and now our boys," said Andrew. "What have we done to deserve this?"

"Our boys, our precious boys are gone; why God, why did this happen?" questioned Jennie.

They both continued to walk through the charred remains. Jennie stepped on the remnants of a letter. She didn't look down and didn't notice the blackened letter. If Jennie had looked down and observed the remains of the charred letter that contained still readable lines, the next several years of her and Andrew's lives would have been altered in the most dramatic way.

"Maybe Maria and the twins are ok. We can't say for sure until we get some details on what exactly happened here," responded Andrew.

Andrew looked across the grounds and noticed a woman watching them from her front yard.

"Jennie, there is a woman in her yard watching us. I think I will go meet her and ask some questions. Maybe you should stay in the car."

"Absolutely not, Andrew. I'm coming with you."

"OK, let's go meet her. Maybe she can tell us what happened here," commented Andrew.

Jennie and Andrew walked across the field to meet the woman. The woman smiled at them and extended her hand out to greet them. "It's terrible, isn't it. Such a tragedy," exclaimed the woman.

"Yes, it is," answered Andrew. "Can you tell us what happened and when?"

The woman went on to explain. "I was out of town when the tragedy happened, but according to the news articles, the fire occurred just three days ago. The fire was a result of the electrical storm and wiring problems in the orphanage. The fire burned so fast that only…." The woman started crying and had to stop to compose herself. "I'm sorry, such a tragedy; there were only two individuals connected to the orphanage that survived the fire, a thirteen-year-old girl and a woman employee that wasn't on site. The girl suffered severe burns but managed somehow to get out. The rest were killed in the fire. According to news articles, there was an explosion inside that collapsed the walls preventing any means of escape."

This was more than Jennie could handle. She broke down in

tears, and Andrew tried to comfort her, but Jennie's emotions were uncontrollable. All Andrew could do was hold Jennie in his arms. After several moments, Andrew composed himself and continued questioning the woman.

"What was the woman's name who was away when the fire struck?" Andrew asked.

"Rhonda, as I recall. She has already gone back east to put this tragedy behind her," the woman responded. "Did you know someone in the orphanage?"

Andrew became very emotional, something that Jennie had not seen before. His arms wrapped around Jennie's shoulders as they were both in tears.

"Yes, we did," was Andrew's reply after a bit.

"I'm so sorry," replied the woman.

"Thank you," responded Andrew. "You mentioned news articles. Was there newspaper coverage on the fire?"

"Yes," responded the woman. "The Daily Sentinel covered the fire. I probably have a copy if you want it." Andrew was very grateful that she had a copy and was willing to share it. The woman went into her house to get the paper. She soon returned, handing the paper to Andrew. Andrew thanked her, and the woman told him that he could keep it. "You two look like such a nice couple. I will be praying for you," stated the woman.

Andrew responded, "Thanks, we could certainly use your prayers. I will leave you with our names and numbers. If you hear any more information or details about this tragedy, please call us."

"I will certainly do that."

Andrew and Jennie left the woman after saying their good-byes and walked back across the field to their car. Before getting in, they took another walk around the charred orphanage.

Both were quiet during the ride home. Andrew held back the tears, but Jennie was unable, with several outbursts of sobbing. Finally, Andrew stopped and also sobbed. They held one another for several moments before resuming the trip.

After arriving home, they sat several moments in silence, and finally, Jennie spoke up. "Oh Andrew, our boys, our precious boys. This has to be God's punishing us for what we have done. What else could it be?" questioned Jennie. "We should have never tried to hide this from your grandparents."

"No, we shouldn't have. You said it before, 'we should have known better,' but now it's too late," responded Andrew. "Whether or not this is God's punishment for us, I can't answer that, but I know someone who can, though."

Jennie asked, "Who do you have in mind?"

"CJ and Sara. They are both dedicated to the Lord, and both can nearly quote the Bible verse by verse," replied Andrew.

CJ and Sara Hilderbrand were indeed very religious and knew the Bible backward and forward. They had been active in their local church in Beaumont for over 50 years and taught Sunday School to nearly every age group in the church. CJ had filled the pulpit on several occasions. They were always there for the church and served the local community, employing several people not only in the area but across the state. The employees had always been treated well and compensated for their loyalty to Hilderbrand enterprises.

CJ had always been the sounding board for any misunderstandings within the church family. On many occasions, he contributed to church members experiencing financial difficulties. His only requirement was that these contributions always remain undivulged, but recipients could usually discern where their good fortune originated.

Jennie rose from the sofa and went to her desk, where she picked up a Bible and began thumbing through the pages. "Yes, I suspect they would have an answer," Jennie commented, "but Andrew, what about CJ's will and your future?"

"I thought about that a lot on our ride home. I prayed a lot also," commented Andrew. "I just feel that the Lord would want us to tell CJ and Sara and ask for forgiveness. As for the future, we put that in God's and CJ's hands. We just need to ask for forgiveness. I have, and I know you have, too."

Jennie answered, "Yes, but what is hard…." Jennie broke down. Andrew went to her and took her in his arms. Jennie continued. "We have lost our two boys, and I may not be able to have children. You know how CJ and Sara wanted us to have children."

"But the doctor didn't rule out the possibility of having children, and adoption is still an option," responded Andrew.

"I know, but I want so much to have our own," Jennie responded.

"Yes, and I do too."

Jennie went on. "When and what exactly do we tell CJ and Sara?"

"The sooner, the better, and we'll tell them exactly what happened."

Jennie then responded, "That we tried to hide it from them and about your concerns over the will?"

"Yes, everything," replied Andrew.

"Andrew, I'm not so sure I can do that, but I know we have to. We need to take a couple more days and be in prayer. It's just too soon for me."

Andrew rose from the sofa and walked across the quiet

room, looking out the window. "OK, we will wait till Sunday. I will call them and invite them over after church on Sunday. That will give us more time to regain our composure and give this some more thought. I'm not sure how to handle the will. I wish I had never heard of that will. It certainly has caused enough family sorrows and now has cost us our sons," Andrew added.

"Andrew, you can't say that. We're completely responsible for our actions and should have prayed more and asked God for wisdom. I know we both have prayed but have we prayed in faith like the Bible tells us to do in the book of James?"

Andrew was silent for several moments and finally responded, "Yes, praying in faith. We both made a bad decision, and you're right. We can't blame CJ and Sara and their will for what happened."

"We shouldn't blame God, either."

"No, we shouldn't, and I pray we never make that mistake again."

"No, Andrew, we won't."

Three agonizing days passed which saw Jennie and Andrew in much prayer and discussion. Both knew that their meeting after church with the elder Hilderbrands would be difficult for them. They would definitely seek God's guidance and put the consequences into His hands.

***

Sunday morning arrived. The message was surely a Godsend and could certainly ease the anticipated tension with CJ and Sara. As Andrew and Jennie were leaving the church, they noticed that there were several members mingling outside the church. They couldn't help but overhear comments about how good the message was. Several women stopped to chat with Jennie. One woman spoke up. "Jennie, we haven't seen you for quite some time. Wasn't the sermon today an inspiring message?"

"Yes, it certainly was, and one perhaps we all needed to hear." The woman looked at Jennie with a puzzled look but didn't comment.

Andrew also stopped to chat with men along the way. He saw CJ visiting with others and began walking over to where he was. They greeted one another with big hugs. "Good sermon wasn't it?" commented Andrew.

"Yes, it certainly was," replied CJ. "At my age, you wouldn't think I could be convicted, but that sermon hit me right between the eyes. Guess I never really thought about forgiveness the way the preacher laid it out today. Dinner at your house, right?"

"That's right."

"What time?"

"How about 4 p.m.?"

"Perfect. I better gather Sara up. I want to discuss the sermon a bit with her. Get her thoughts."

CJ left Andrew and walked over to where Sara was visiting with other ladies. Andrew went to find Jennie, who was visiting with other women. "You ready, Jennie? We better get going. CJ and Sara will be over at 4 p.m."

"Oh my, yes, we had," replied Jennie.

Jennie waved goodbye to the ladies and went to the car, where Andrew was waiting. They left the church. Neither said a word for several moments; both were in deep concentration. After arriving home, they changed into casual clothes, and Jennie began preparing for their evening meal with CJ and

Sara.

Dinner wasn't weighing on Jennie's mind nearly as much as the anticipated discussion that was to follow.

That afternoon, Jennie noticed Andrew sitting in the large leather chair in their living room. He seemed to be in deep meditation and thumbing through his Bible. "What're you doing?" Jennie asked.

"Looking for some passages on forgiveness. Seems today's message struck a nerve with a lot of people."

Jennie responded, "It was a wonderful message. I have been thinking about it ever since we left the church. It really got my attention."

"Yes, and mine also. Evidently, it hit a nerve with CJ as well."

"How do you know, Andrew?"

"CJ told me after church, something about being old and convicted. What perfect timing for a sermon on forgiveness, especially for what is coming up this evening."

"About those passages…" Jennie walked over to the end table, picked up her Bible, and sat down by Andrew. Andrew was glancing at her Bible and noticed a lot of notes on the pages.

"Looks like you use that Bible a lot," commented Andrew.

"I do. In fact, I've been doing a devotion every morning after you go to the office, and I try and read every night before retiring."

"I had no idea," responded Andrew.

Jennie continued, "The Bible is the inspired word of God and is full of passages on grace, love, and forgiveness. Here, let me show you a couple of my favorite passages on forgiveness." Jennie turned the pages and pointed out the first passage: "But if we confess our sins to him, he is faithful and just to forgive us our sins and to cleanse us from all wickedness.[7]"

Andrew commented that he knew that one but had forgotten where it was. Jennie stated her favorite passage on forgiveness was found in the book of Luke.

Andrew said, "Don't tell me," and recited the verse: "Do not judge others and you will not be judged. Do not condemn others, for it will all come back against you. Forgive others, and you will be forgiven.[8]"

"Why, Andrew, I am proud of you."

"Jennie, this is good. Starting tonight, I will spend more time in God's word. We should do a devotion together." Jennie's face lit up with a big smile, and she responded to Andrew's idea.

"Oh, Andrew, I would love to have a time of devotion together. As I remember, my mother and father spent a lot of time in God's word together. I really miss that."

It was nearing 4 p.m. when their doorbell rang. It was CJ and Sara, arriving right on time as usual. Andrew opened the door and welcomed the couple.

CJ asked, "Are we late?"

"Right on time," Andrew responded. "Jennie is putting the finishing touches on dinner. Pot roast and vegetables; your favorites, as I recall."

CJ responded, "You recalled right, and I am ready for it."

They all gathered at the table as Jennie served. Andrew asked CJ to say the blessing. Everyone bowed their heads in prayer. CJ began, "Heavenly Father, we are thankful for this day and the many blessings we receive. We are thankful for the food we are about to receive and ask that you bless this food to our bodies and the hands that prepared it, and yes, Father, we thank you for the wonderful message we heard this morning,

7 New Living Translation, 1 John 1:9
8 New Living Translation, Luke 6:37

and Father, may we always remember Your forgiveness that you extend to us in Jesus Holy name, Amen."

"Amen," they all said together. A look of contentment was obvious on the faces of Jennie and Andrew.

Casual conversation continued during the meal between the family as they all reflected on and discussed the morning service. Jennie couldn't help noticing the facial expressions, especially of Andrew.

Afterward, CJ commented, "That was one of the best pot roasts I've had in a long time, maybe even as good as Sara's."

"Oh, CJ, that wasn't necessary." Jennie left to clean up and do the dishes while the other three retired to the living room.

Sara left and joined Jennie in the kitchen, where they commenced casual conversation about the morning sermon.

"CJ, after church, you made some comments on the sermon this morning."

"Yes, I did. Sara and I discussed that sermon this afternoon at great length. It was a powerful one, wasn't it?"

"Yes, it was," exclaimed Andrew. "That is the main reason Jennie and I invited you two over this afternoon. Jennie and I want to share with you and Sara something that has been tearing us apart for the last nine months. Let's wait until they join us."

After a few moments passed, Sara and Jennie came back into the living room. CJ looked at Sara with a concerned look. Andrew noticed Jennie already had tears in her eyes.

It was 6 p.m. when Andrew started his confession. "We have sinned against you, and we have sinned against God, and all we can do is ask for forgiveness from you and Sara. We both have asked for God's forgiveness for the terrible thing we have done. Now we want to ask you for forgiveness.

"I will start from the beginning and tell you two the whole story, exactly what happened." After a minute of total silence, Andrew went on. He proceeded to tell all the details of the previous several months. He explained how he and Jennie had covered up Jennie's pregnancy while doing her project at the marine lab, the delivery of twin boys, and the complications that could possibly affect natural delivery in the future. Maria, Jennie's friend's, involvement was detailed.

It was extremely difficult for Andrew to continue, but he knew he had to. Andrew explained how Maria was to contact them daily on how the twins were doing. "Maria phoned us every day for several days to let us know the twins were doing okay. Then the calls stopped. We had no calls for two days. We tried to contact Maria and even tried to call the orphanage."

Andrew proceeded after several moments of silence, and both he and Jennie had to compose themselves for what was to come. Andrew indicated that both he and Jennie were very concerned and knew they had to return to Baja to find out what had happened and the reason for the discontinued phone calls. He described in detail what they found on their arrival at the orphanage. He detailed the conversation with the older woman that lived near the facility. Nothing was left out of Andrew's story. However, there was no mention of the Hilderbrand will in the discourse. After several moments of silence, it was now indicated 7 p.m. Andrew continued and brought the confession to a close.

"Well, that's the whole story. We wouldn't blame either of you if you never forgave us. We will have to live with this for the rest of our lives and pray that God will forgive us. The fact that Jennie may never bear another child hurts the most. I guess this is God's way of punishing us."

CJ responded, "First of all, Sara and I are so sorry this has happened. I only wish you and Jennie had confided in us sooner. If this is God's punishment, I don't know. One thing I do know for sure: God has forgiven you and Jennie, and rest assured, Sara and I also forgive you. You two are all Sara and I have left, and no matter what has happened, Sara and I both love you very much. About children, should Jennie not be able to have natural births, you can always adopt. You both need to be in earnest prayer about this. Jennie, don't give up hope. We all know that God moves in mysterious ways. It may take time and a lot of prayer, but I believe God has a plan for you two, and we can't imagine what that plan is."

"Oh, CJ, what can we say?" Jennie replied. "You and Sara are such wonderful people. Andrew and I have already discussed adopting. We know how you wanted grandchildren, and we want so bad to have children."

"Perhaps this is not the appropriate time, but I know you two know about a will that was written up years ago. That will probably cost Sara and I two children and a lot of the heart-aches and now this. Sara and I had that will voided several years ago. I want this topic dropped and forgotten about. We all need to move forward with our lives and live with an attitude of love and joy and seek God's will for our lives."

After CJ's response, they gathered in a circle in the middle of the living room, held hands, and lowered their heads in prayer. They stood there several moments praying silently, and then CJ closed in prayer.

CJ and Sara picked up their coats from the hall closet and went to the front entry. But before they left, CJ turned back to Andrew and Jennie to share a few last words. "Jennie, thank you for the wonderful dinner. You two hang in there, and our prayers are with you."

Andrew and Jennie escorted CJ and Sara to the door and said their goodnights. Jennie added, "Thank you so much for your forgiveness and words of encouragement."

After CJ and Sara left, Andrew and Jennie embraced silently for several moments. Then Jennie commented, "They are such lovely people, and I am so proud to be a part of this family. They both have so much wisdom."

After their evening encounter with CJ and Sara, the lives of both Andrew and Jennie had some dramatic changes. Andrew settled into his position with Hilderbrand Enterprises and was officially appointed CEO of the corporation. Jennie utilized her master's degree at a nearby laboratory. They were not able to accommodate their adoption plans because they wanted a set of twins. The thought of losing their twin sons weighed very heavy on their hearts, and they had been unsuccessful with natural childbirth. Both had settled into their local church and were now teaching Sunday School classes.

CHAPTER NINE

$\mathcal{T}$welve years later, the small town of Beaumont had grown in population by 7000. The park trail that Andrew and Jennie still jogged had been expanded as well as the park itself. Hilderbrand Enterprises had also grown substantially in size, adding several hundred additional employees. Andrew's promotion to CEO had proven to be a wise decision, and he had established an excellent rapport with the employees. Since his promotion, his out-of-town travel was greatly reduced. CJ wasn't seen in the home office nearly as frequently. Jennie had discontinued her work at the lab and now focused on community projects.

Jennie's parents were able to leave their mission field to spend three weeks with her and Andrew. They shared their experiences and how it was a real blessing to see so many come to the Lord. Jennie, however, made no mention of the mistake that she and Andrew had made years earlier. To her surprise, no mention of children ever came up.

Because of growth, Beaumont was now the home of three new churches. A mission center had been established, which provided for a number of citizens of all ages. Although much growth had occurred in the community and safety was not an issue, residents always seemed to have time to enjoy a friendly conversation with whomever they met, regardless of location.

One addition to the community that had met with considerable approval was a small mobile hot dog cart operated by a young entrepreneur known only as Billy. He just happened to be a Godly individual who was well respected by all who purchased hot dogs from his stand. Anyone who purchased and ate a hot dog with all the trimmings from Billy was hooked.

It is at this hotdog stand that our story becomes more intriguing when a young boy approaches the cart.

"Hey bro, how are you?" questioned Billy. "Haven't seen you in a couple days. "Are you getting tired of eating my dogs, or are you getting fed too well at the mission?"

The boy named Jay answered, "No, I haven't been to the mission for a long time."

Billy looked a bit puzzled and asked, "Where ya been hangin' out?"

"Been hangin' out in a big house across town."

"What kind of big house?" Billy asked.

"I'd rather not say."

"Ah, come on, you can trust me, and I won't say a word. You have been my best salesman, you know; telling people that I have the best dogs in the city has really improved my business, and dogs are on me, bro."

"Thanks, you really do have good dogs, and I tell everyone I meet."

"OK, bro, where are you staying?"

Jay hesitated, "Well, I guess you won't tell anybody."

"You can trust me, Jay. After all, I don't want to lose my best salesman."

"Well, okay then. I've been living in a church."

Chuckling, Billy responded, "A what?"

"A church. I found a way to get in and out without being seen. They always serve food after the preacher quits yappin'."

"Preaching, Jay, not yappin'. I go to church, you know. You need to respect preachers."

"Yeah, I guess so. It's just I don't know what he's talking about most of the time."

"Most of the time; aay, do you understand anything the pastor says?"

"Yes, a little bit."

Billy asked Jay, "Do you own a Bible?"

Jay responded, "No, I don't need one. There are lots of Bibles in the big house, I mean church."

"Well, Jay, we need to sit down and have a talk one of these times."

"Yeah, I guess we should."

A young couple with two small children walked up to the cart. "Four hot dogs, please," requested the customer. The man noticed Jay near the cart. "Hey kid, aren't you the one who told us about these great hot dogs?"

"Maybe. Well, Billy, I better get going. Got a couple lawns I promised to mow this afternoon."

"Well, see ya, bro."

Jay left on his bike and headed down the street.

After receiving the hot dogs, the man told Billy he was sure that Jay was the kid that told him about the hot dogs. Billy responded that he probably was. "Jay tells a lot of people about my dogs and has been a real asset to me. I don't have to advertise. Jay does all that for me. What's very odd, though, is that most of the time, he is very shy and not very talkative."

"That's strange for a kid his age."

"Yes, it is," responded Billy. "Most kids his age usually won't stop talking, and it's difficult to get a word in edgewise. At least he talks enough to send customers my way."

Jay arrived at a large home with immaculate landscaping and walked up the sidewalk to the front door. He rang the doorbell, and a woman opened her door. "Good afternoon, Jay. I forgot this was lawnmowing day."

"That's okay."

"You know where the mower is. I won't keep you."

Jay went to the storage shed behind the house and got the mower out, checked the gas and oil levels, and then began mowing the lawns. After he was finished, he put the mower away, went to the front door, and rang the bell. "I'm finished. I used the last of the oil and may need some more after two or three cuttings. The mower uses more oil than it should."

"You know, Jay, that is a very old mower. Next week you will be using a new mower. How does that sound?"

"That will be great!"

"Jay, as I recall, you have been mowing my lawn for about three years."

"Yes, I think so."

"You have done such a good job. I'll tell you what, starting today, I'm going to start paying you $40 rather than the $20 I have been giving you."

Jay responded, "Wow, thank you, Mrs. Simpson, but that's too much."

She replied, "Our lawn has never looked as good as it does since you have been taking care of it. In fact, several of our friends have commented and have inquired about you. I'm sure if you were available, I could line you up with more lawn jobs."

"Gee, thanks; I have several now but could always do some

more."

Mrs. Simpson asked, "Swell. How do I contact you?"

Jay replied, "That may be a problem. Maybe you can tell your friends that I would be available to do more lawns. They need to know, though, that I don't have a mower, and they would have to supply one for me. Gee, Mrs. Simpson, I sure would appreciate more lawn jobs, and thank you for the pay increase."

Jay got onto his bike and started down the street with a big smile on his face. More lawn jobs would certainly help contribute to his plans for the future.

After Jay left, Mrs. Simpson thought, *What a nice young lad. I certainly would like to know who his parents are to compliment them on their son. Come to think about it, I really don't know that much about the lad at all.*

***

*A*cross town from where Jay was mowing, another boy by the name of Mick was mowing an older gentleman's lawn. The gentleman was on crutches, and it was quite evident that he was not able to mow his own lawn.

"The lawn really looks good, Mick. I'm sure glad you showed up last week. How long you been mowing lawns?"

Mick replied, "I guess about three years now."

"Well, how did you get started?"

"I just started knocking on doors and asking the owner if they needed their lawn mown? I now have several customers."

In response, the old man said, "You do a great job. Upon opening his wallet, the man took out some cash. Here's $20. See you next week. You keep doing such a fine job, and I will increase the amount."

"Thanks, I'll be here."

Mick got on his bike and rode down the street. He rode to a small house next to a very large church. He was met by an older man who asked him if he got his customer's lawn taken care of. Mick responded, "Yep. The fellow even told me that he would pay me more if I keep doing a good job."

The older man said, "You know, I've been the custodian at this church for over 30 years and never met a young lad quite like you. I remember the day I caught you sneaking food down into the basement of the church. You reminded me of myself when I was young. How long had you been living in the church anyway?"

Mick replied, "I don't know for sure, maybe three or four years."

"Well, you can stay with me a little while longer until I move up to Oregon. I hear they will tear this house down in a few months."

Being quite concerned, Mick rubbed his chin. "Why are they doing that?"

"Guess they think they need more room."

"You won't tell them about my living in the church, will you?" Mick questioned.

"Don't you worry, lad. This will always be our little secret. I am worried about you though, you with no parents. What are you going to do?"

Mick replied, "I'll be ok; I will find someplace." Mick had a smile on his face, looked up, and rubbed his chin. "Maybe I'll find another church."

"You know Mick, with no parents, maybe you would like to move up to Oregon with me. It will be a while, but you sure are welcome to go with me."

"I'll think about it. Thanks for the offer. I really don't have any reasons to stay around here."

The next day was Sunday. Jay approached the church and hid his bike in the shrubs behind the church as he had done on many previous Sundays. He then went down a few steps and cautiously looked all around. He lifted a brick and got a key which unlocked a side door that entered the basement area of the church. An older gentleman was quietly watching every move that Jay was making. Just before Jay entered the church, the older man snuck up behind him and grabbed his arm. Jay turned around with a look of surprise and his mouth wide open. The man put his finger to his lips, telling Jay to be silent. They both entered the church. Jay was still shaken from the encounter, wondering what would come next.

"Don't be scared," said the man. "I'm the groundskeeper and church janitor. I've seen you in the church for a long time and always wondered how you got in. I've never seen you with anyone and never have seen you come in the front doors of the church like everyone else does. Who are your parents?"

Jay looked down and hesitantly replied, "I don't have any parents, or if I do, I've never known them."

The man answered, "I suspected that. Do you have a name?"

"I'm just called Jay. I think my real name was Jake, but I like Jay better."

"You been living in the church then?"

"Yes," replied Jay, "but I guess not anymore, though."

"I live in a small house next to the church," stated the man. Would you like to stay with me until we find something better? And by the way, I like Jay better, too." From that day forward, Jake officially became known as Jay.

"I guess so," replied Jay. "You won't tell on me, will you?"

The man went on, "No, but there are a couple rules to follow."

"What are they?"

"You have to attend church here every Sunday."

"I've already been doing that."

"Yes, I suppose you have, alright."

"What is the other rule?"

"I don't want you to tell anyone that I have known what you have been doing. We just keep this between the two of us. Deal?"

"Deal," Jay answered. "By the way, what is your name?"

"Mr. Croft."

After Jay's encounter with Mr. Croft, he proceeded up the stairs to the balcony, where he always sat during the morning service. Jay, although only twelve years of age, always felt that since he was secretly staying in the church for shelter and often food, the least he could do was to listen to the singing and sermon. He even found himself singing some of the old hymns, and of course, he had his favorites, including 'Victory in Jesus' and 'When the Roll is Called up Yonder.' He loved those two oldies. He really didn't understand the sermons, but from bits and pieces he heard, he was aware of who Jesus was.

This Sunday found Jay more attentive than usual since meeting Mr. Croft. He was certain that Mr. Croft would keep his word and not reveal who he was, but still, there was some apprehension on his part. Jay sat in his usual spot and watched the congregation arrive for the Sunday morning service. He noticed the woman playing music at the organ and the warm smile on her face. Her hands glided ever so smoothly over the keyboard. He then noticed a young couple and saw that they sat by an older couple in the pews. Jay's eyes were glued on the young couple, and he thought, *Wonder why I haven't noticed her before. Boy, is she pretty.* He continued looking around the church and then to the balcony opposite where he sat. He spotted another kid walking toward him. The boy approached Jay and sat down.

Jay spoke to him. "Hi. Haven't seen you here before."

"My first time here," responded the kid.

Jay asked, "Are you new in town?"

"Nah," the kid said. "I live across town; I'm just church hoppin'."

Jay replied, "Church hoppin'? What's that?"

"Oh, trying out different churches."

"Well, this is a good church. I've gone here for years. Are your mom and dad here?"

The kid, looking down sadly and slow to answer, said, "I don't have a mom and dad."

Jay was astonished, "What a coincidence; neither do I."

"You don't either? What's your name?"

"Jay," was the response.

"Mine is Mick."

"Where do you live?" asked Mick.

"I've been living in the church basement, but starting tomorrow, I'll be living with the church janitor who lives next door. He's really nice."

"You've been living in this church? That's funny; I used to live in a church across town. But now I live with an old man who lives by the church. He told me a few days ago he was moving to Oregon. I'll probably have to find another place to live. That's why I'm checking out other churches. I still have some time, though, before he moves."

"Do you like baseball?" Jay asked.

"I love it. It's my favorite sport."

"What position do you play?"

"I like to pitch."

"Really, I do, too. We should get together sometime and play catch. There is a park with ball diamonds just down the street from here. We can meet there and play. Might even get in a pickup game. They have them there a lot."

"Wow, I would love that. That would be cool."

"Let's meet there next Saturday."

"OK."

Jay dropped the baseball talk and nudged Mick, "The preacher is starting. We better be quiet and pretend we are listening."

CHAPTER TEN

$\mathcal{T}$oday was Saturday, and it was the day of the big championship game between Andrew's team and the team coached by his best friend, Carl. Both coaches had been ribbing each other all week and had made a side bet on who would win. The loser would have to treat the winning coach and his wife to dinner.

Andrew was in the living room dressed in his favorite shorts, team jersey, and baseball cap. He made one final appeal to Jennie. "Sure you can't come to our game today? It's the final game of the season, and Carl's and my team are tied for first. It's a championship game and should be a dandy. We both have the two best pitchers in the league."

"Oh, Andrew, I'm so sorry. I wish I could, but I promised the ladies at the church I would help set up the bake and craft sale at the church this morning," Jennie replied. "Believe me, I would much prefer the game. Those ladies are so picky, and it takes them forever to decide on prices. I will be finished in time to be at the BBQ and swim party."

"Well, okay," as he gave her a peck on the cheek and headed to the front door with his bag of baseball gear and ball glove. Just as he was leaving, the phone rang.

"Hello," answered Jennie.

"Hello, Jennie, this is Mrs. Wilson. Is Andrew there?" Andrew put his finger over his mouth and shook his head no.

Jennie replied, "He's just leaving for the game. Is something wrong?"

"Jackson woke up this morning and has the flu and won't be able to play this morning."

"Oh, dear," Jennie replied. "Andrew received another call this morning, and Richard will not be there either. I sure hope Jackson gets better soon."

"Thanks, and I hope so, too."

Andrew rubbed his forehead and just shook his head in disbelief. "This is not good. Our team is down to nine players. Thank God that they are the best nine. We can't postpone. Today is it." Andrew left the house and put the equipment in the car. Jennie walked out with him. "Good luck. I will be praying for you."

"Thanks, we could sure use it at this point."

Andrew arrived at the park and noticed the stands were already filling up with family members and friends. Parents of players were taking pictures and visiting with other team parents and families. Players were getting warmed up and playing catch.

Mick and Jay were off to the sidelines in their tees and cut-offs. Both boys were about the same size and age as Andrew's team members. The two coaches got their teams together and went over the rules with the three umpires.

Andrew looked toward the parking lot with an anxious look on his face. The other team coach was doing the same as well as a lot of pacing. Andrew walked over to Carl and then took a final look toward the parking lot. There he saw one of his players approaching on crutches.

"Well, Carl, this doesn't look good for our team. I have only nine players, and now my pitcher is on crutches." Andrew addressed his player. "Jeff, what happened to you?"

Jeff replied, "Sorry, coach, I had a little accident this morning and sprained my ankle. I really feel bad letting the team down."

"Accidents will happen, and I'm sorry about the ankle."

Mick and Jay continued playing catch. They were able to hear the conversations that were going on.

"This is really crazy. I can't believe this is happening. Our last game, too. I got three phone calls last night from players who were sick, and one of them was my pitcher. His mother said he might be ready for today's game, but he hasn't shown up," remarked Carl. "That leaves our team with eight players also. Is this a coincidence or what?"

Mick and Jay looked at each other with snide grins. They both stepped closer to the two coaches, still discussing the situation. Andrew stood there with a frown on his face questioning what to do. "Then we both have eight players, and neither of us has a pitcher," Andrew said to Carl, "I guess we can call it even and end the season in a tie for first place."

"Yeah, I guess that will have to do," Carl commented. "I guess you and I could be our team pitchers, and at least we can play a game."

Mick, who was listening, spoke up. "Hey, mister, my friend and I could play. We both can pitch."

Andrew and Carl moved aside and discussed the situation out of earshot of Mick and Jay and the other team members. After the two coaches had some time to think about it, Andrew approached Mick, asking him, "How old are you and your friend?"

Mick replied, "We are both twelve."

"Do you live around here?"

"Yea, we both live across town."

"What's you and your friend's name?" Andrew asked.

Pausing for a moment, Mick replied, "I'm Mickey, and that's Jay."

Andrew rubbed his chin and looked at both boys for several moments. He focused on Mick and had a flashback of himself when he was young. He then commented, "Hmm, Mickey and Jay, huh?" He turned to Carl. "Well, Carl, what do you think? Should we let these two lads play?"

"Yea, why not? I have an extra team shirt. How about you?"

"Yea, I do too. Let's check with the umps and tell them what we are doing."

Andrew and Carl conferred with the umpires, and it was agreed to let Mickey and Jay play. They motioned for the two boys to join them with the umpires at home plate.

"Well, you boys can play," Andrew told them, "Mickey, you pitch for my team, and Jay can pitch for Carl's team. Take your tees off and put these team jerseys on."

Mick and Jay went over to the sidelines and put the team jerseys on over their tees. The two coaches looked at each other and shook their heads. They gathered at home plate with the umpires for the coin flip to decide which team was to be the home team. Andrew won the coin toss, and his team took the field.

The umpire yelled, "Play ball!" The parents started cheering for their kids, and all eyes were on the players as the first batter stepped to the plate. Mick looked at the catcher and threw the first pitch. The batter stood in amazement as the pitch hit the catcher's glove. Both coaches stared in awe at the pitch. The umpire yelled, "Strike one," his mouth open and a look of surprise on his face.

The catcher just shook his head as he said, "Ouch!" Mick delivered the next pitch, and the batter swung way late.

Umpire, "Strike two."

Mick hesitated, wound up, and delivered the next pitch. The batter swung late and the umpire called "Strike three."

Mick struck out all three batters.

Jay took the mound and threw some warm-up pitches. Andrew's first player stepped up to the plate, and Jay threw the first pitch. The batter watched the ball sail into the catcher's glove.

Umpire, "Strike one!"

The batter commented, "Man, he throws fast!"

Jay delivered the next pitch.

Umpire, "Strike two!"

Next pitch, "Strike three! You're out!"

Jay struck out all three batters. The umpire called Andrew and Carl over to talk behind home plate. "Who are these two boys? Do they live around here? I have never seen either one of them before. You sure they're only twelve years old?"

"That's what they said, and they both live across town," said Carl. "They must be new to the community."

"This is the first time Carl or I have seen either one of them. They both have obviously played a lot before."

"That's for sure," commented Carl, shaking his head in disbelief.

The game entered the last inning. Neither team had scored a run. There were two outs, and Jay was the next batter. The fans were hollering and really into the game. Mick was getting ready to deliver the pitch. "Come on, Jay, get a hit, get us started," hollered Carl.

Mick looked at Jay and delivered the pitch. Jay focused intently on the pitch, swung, and the bat cracked. The ball sailed over the left-field fence. The team in the dugout went wild, the fans started hollering. Andrew stared at the ball sailing over the fence. Mick turned and watched the ball go over the fence and then watched Jay round the bases. As Jay crossed home plate, he was mobbed by his teammates.

Andrew's team huddled in the dugout. "OK, guys, they scored a run; we still can do it. Start us off, Toby."

Jay struck out Toby.

The next batter grounded out to the second baseman.

Mick stepped up to the plate. Jay looked at Mick with a glare in his eyes and a big grin on his face. The fans and both coaches were focused on the pitcher and the batter.

"Come on, Mick, you can do it," hollered Andrew.

Jay wound up and delivered the pitch. Mick swung and made contact. The ball sailed over the left-field fence, and Mick circled the bases. The fans erupted in cheers. Andrew and his players poured out of the dugout to meet Mick at home plate.

The next batter struck out, and the game ended in a tie.

All three umpires gathered with the coaches at the sidelines, and the home plate umpire commented, "I sure wish we didn't have a time restriction. I would love to see these two pitchers duel it out some more. I have never seen two young boys with the talent I have witnessed here today. If they are indeed twelve years of age, mark my words with proper coaching, both boys will surely be offered a free ride at major universities. You two coaches keep your eyes on them. Unbelievable is all I can say."

Andrew and Carl gathered their respective teams at the

sidelines. "Well, guys, what a game. We end the season tied." Andrew commented. "Don't forget the teams meet in the park later this afternoon for the BBQ and swimming."

Both coaches informed their team members they could keep their jerseys and would be receiving new ones the next season. Andrew called Mick and Jay over to where he and Carl were handing out team jerseys. "You two boys can keep those jerseys. You boys earned them today. You are sure welcome to join us later for an end of the year barbecue and team swim party."

Mick and Jay both replied softly, "Yeh, maybe we can."

The players all left to join their parents, and Andrew and Carl met at their cars.

"I can't believe what I just saw," commented Andrew.

"Me neither," responded Carl. "Those two kids were amazing. We need to find out where they live and make sure we get them back next season. "

Andrew shook his head. "Yes, for sure. There is just something about those two that..." Andrew paused and looked puzzled.

"What?" responded Carl.

Andrew continued. "I don't know. I just have this funny feeling that I should know them, kind of a gut feeling. It's hard to explain. Well, I better get home. A lot to do before the BBQ. I hope those boys show up for the party, but you know, Carl, by the way, they both quietly responded to our invitation, I somehow don't believe they will."

Both got into their cars and left the ballpark.

Andrew headed home. He and Jennie both arrived home at the same time. "So, how was the craft sale, Jennie?"

"Good, same ole, same ole, lots of lady gossip and, you know, chatter. How was the game? Did you win?"

"You won't believe what happened. Let's go inside, and I'll explain," replied Andrew.

Andrew and Jennie entered the living room and sat on their large chairs facing their bay window. After sitting for a second, Andrew stood up and started pacing around the room. Andrew continued. "To start with, we didn't win. The game ended in a tie, but that's just the beginning. Carl and I got to the ballpark and found out we both only had eight players, and neither of us had our star pitchers. We were about ready to call the game off when these two boys showed up." Andrew continued filling in all the details of the game. He continued his pacing around the room, detailing what happened with animated motion.

Jennie exclaimed, "That's incredible. Did the boys say where they live, who their parents are, did they look like brothers? Andrew, we must find those boys. The names, the age, could it be possible?"

Andrew exclaimed, "I know, and I've been thinking the same thing. We know the orphanage burned down and there were only two survivors; at least that's the story. All the records were lost but could there have been some more survivors? We need to revisit that orphanage site. Perhaps we missed something and assumed all the children were lost in the fire. Maybe some nearby residents can give us some information. As you recall, we only spoke with one older lady, and she was not at home when the fire occurred."

"Oh, Andrew, we need to pray about this."

Andrew added, "Yes, we do and then take a road trip in the near future."

"Will the boys be at the BBQ?"

"I invited them. Let's just hope they come. I would like to

ask them a few questions. I would also like for you to meet them."

That afternoon, all the players and parents arrived at the park for the BBQ and swimming party. Andrew mingled with the parents and set up the grills. The boys had all gone swimming when they first arrived. Carl approached Andrew., "Any sign of the star pitchers?"

"Not yet," Andrew exclaimed. "As I said after the game, I have a gut feeling they won't show up. Neither of them was very positive when I gave them the invitation. There's just something about those two that I can't put my finger on. I keep wondering why both boys put the jerseys over their tee shirts, especially since it was so warm."

"Um, right," Carl said, shaking his head. "That was rather odd, now that you mention it."

***

The BBQ ended, and everyone prepared to leave, shaking hands and wishing parents and team members a good rest of the summer. Jennie and Andrew were the last ones to leave. As they walked to their car, Andrew was noticeably disappointed. Jennie asked, "They didn't show up, did they?"

"No, they didn't, but it doesn't surprise me."

CHAPTER ELEVEN

Two weeks later, Jay was pedaling his bike through the park with a sack of pop cans in his basket. He was gazing around the park and did not pay much attention to his surroundings. He didn't see Andrew jogging towards him on the same path from the opposite direction. Andrew glanced down to see that his shoe was untied and stopped to tie it. Jay, not watching the path ahead but looking for pop cans, did not see Andrew on his knee tying his shoe. The collision that followed resulted in quite a scene. Jay flew over the handlebars, Andrew went backward in a somersault, and pop cans were strewn all over the pathway. Andrew, dazed, got up and saw Jay on the ground. "Are you ok, man?" Andrew asked. "I should have been paying more attention."

"Yeah, me, too, but I'm ok."

"Are you sure?"

"I'm alright." Jay looked at Andrew and noticed some blood on Andrew's leg.

"Hey, mister, your leg is bleeding." Andrew looked at his leg and noticed a trickle of blood running down his leg. He produced a tissue from his pocket and wiped the blood off.

Andrew commented, "It's just a scratch, nothing serious." Andrew looked at Jay and put his hand on his shoulder. Jay looked away. "Hmm, you look familiar. Now I remember. You're the kid who pitched for the team we played in the park a couple of weeks ago."

"Yeah, it was me. You sure had a good pitcher."

"You both were good; no, not good; superb," Andrew remarked. "Where did you learn to pitch like that?"

"Oh, I don't know. Just luck, I guess, playing with friends."

"Where do you live anyway? And by the way, what did you say your name was?" Andrew knew full well what Jay's name was and was very curious how the boy would respond.

Jay looked away and mumbled his name, but Andrew didn't hear him. "I have to go, mister. Sorry I ran into you."

Jay picked up his bike and sack of cans, climbed on his bike, and headed down the path.

"By the way," Andrew hollered, "my name is Andrew."

***

Jennie was across town jogging on another recently constructed park trail in shorts and a T-top. She listened to music on earphones as she jogged. Mick was riding a bike on the path with his basket full of pop cans and turned his head to look at two teenage girls that smiled at him. Mick and Jennie collided with one another, sending Jennie for a loop. Mick fell from his bike and lay on the ground, a bit dazed. Jennie, also a bit dazed, got up from the ground and brushed herself off. She looked at Mick, who was now standing by his downed bike.

"Hey, young man, you need to watch where you're going," said Jennie. "Are you ok?"

"Yea, I'm ok. Ma'am, I'm really sorry, but…"

"I know, I know," stated Jennie. "Those two girls were cute, and they had their eyes on you. You were just being a boy."

"Yeah, they sure were cute, weren't they? Are you alright?" asked Mick.

"Yes, I'm fine," exclaimed Jennie. "I haven't seen you around here before. Do you live nearby?"

"I live across town with a friend of mine in a big rock house."

Jennie walked toward Mick and intently looked him up and down. "You look like somebody I should know. Do you have a brother?"

"No."

"What did you say your name was?"

"I didn't say, but it's Micky; I better get going. Sorry I ran into you." Mick picked up his bike and scattered pop cans.

Jennie watched Mick as he rode down the path and disappeared out of sight. Jennie rubbed her chin and began jogging toward home.

She arrived home and entered the front door to find Andrew sitting at a table with a soda in his hand, looking at a photo album. "What are you looking at?" asked Jennie.

"I'm looking at some old albums of my dad and me. You remember that kid that pitched for Carl's team a few weeks ago?"

"Yes, I remember you telling me about him," replied Jennie, "and how good he was."

"Well, I saw him again today," exclaimed Andrew. "Not the most pleasant meeting. In fact, he ran into me on his bike and threw me for a loop."

Jennie's mouth flew open, and she gasped in disbelief. That's impossible. "Are you kidding me? I don't believe it."

"What do you mean you don't believe it? It happened, and

here's proof." Andrew pulled up his pant leg and showed Jennie the scrape on his leg.

Jennie went on. "No, no, that isn't what I meant. I believe you, but this is crazy. The same thing happened to me just a few minutes ago across town in the new park while I was jogging home. Some kid who said his name was Mickey was gawking at a couple of cute girls and ran into me with his bike. His sack of pop cans flew all over. Fortunately, neither of us was hurt, just a bit shaken."

"What, did you say, pop cans? Now, isn't that a coincidence? The kid that ran me over was also collecting pop cans. Did you say his name was Mickey?"

"That's what he said. Evidently, he lives across town with a friend. Oh yeah, near a big house."

Andrew walked around the room before returning to the desk and re-opening the photo album. "Was the kid, I mean Mickey, about twelve or thirteen years old?"

Jennie responded, "I would say about that."

Andrew went on, "The two boys that pitched a few weeks ago both said they were twelve and their names were Jay and Mickey. This has to be more than a coincidence. They must be the same two boys."

"Oh, Andrew, what are you thinking?"

"I don't know what to think, but have a look at the pictures of my father and me when we were about the age of those two boys."

Jennie went over to the table and stared at the album. She turned the pages and stopped abruptly, clasping her hand over her mouth and looking at Andrew. "This picture, Andrew, this is you, and that boy could be your double."

Andrew turned the album pages rapidly toward the front,

pointing to another picture. "Look at this picture of CJ. He was fourteen years old in this picture. Jay looks a lot like CJ. Those two boys fascinated me the first time I saw them. I just couldn't put my finger on it, but now… no, it couldn't be. Our boys were both killed in the fire over twelve years ago. They are just friends, or at least that is what they said. They could have passed for brothers."

"Could it be possible? I mean, could our boys still be alive?"

"I can't answer that," responded Andrew. "It has been over twelve years since that tragic fire but was something over-looked? We have got to get to the bottom of this. There are just too many things that are not adding up right now. We have looked all over town for those boys, and there has been no sign of either one of them. They can't both just disappear."

"No, they sure can't. We now know for sure they live in this town, either in a big house or near a big house."

"You know, Jennie, it's time for that road trip. I now wished we had gone sooner."

"Yes, let's leave early in the morning."

"My exact thoughts. We can discuss our course of action on the road. I'll call CJ later and let him know we'll be going out of town for a couple days."

Andrew and Jennie rushed around the house, throwing some items in an overnight bag. They both double-checked their items and were satisfied the necessary essentials were included.

"Got everything I need," exclaimed Andrew.

"Me too."

Later that evening, after their Bible reading, they recalled and discussed the events of the day and looked at the photo album with renewed hope. "Andrew, I just can't believe what happened to us today and nearly simultaneous. Is God trying to show us something?"

"I think He might be, and I guess we may find out in the next couple of days."

"Did you call CJ?"

"Called him earlier this evening. I told him we should be back in a day or two. CJ said he and Sara were going to take a couple weeks and fly out to see some old friends in Wisconsin. I guess we are ready to skedaddle and hopefully finally get some answers."

"Oh, Andrew, this is exciting."

CHAPTER TWELVE

$\mathcal{E}$arly the next morning, Andrew and Jennie left the house, and Andrew drove the shortest route to the orphanage site. They again discussed all the recent encounters with the two boys and all the possible scenarios and what-ifs.

Upon arriving at the orphanage, they found that the site had been cleared. In its place were several graves with headstones, as well as the remains of a large rock cross. They exited the car and slowly walked around the area as they looked at the graves and cross. "Are you sure this is where the orphanage was?" stated Andrew. "There were only three houses here before."

"Positive, Andrew. I will never forget that cross and the verse that was engraved on the base."

"What was it?" asked Andrew.

"Go over to the cross, and I will give you the verse and quote it."

Andrew went over to the cross and looked at the verse while Jennie quoted it. "I can do all things through Him who gives me strength.[9]"

"Well, there's no doubt that this is where the orphanage

was. Let's just hope that someone who lived in one of those homes when the fire occurred is still there," suggested Andrew. "As I remember, no one was present at any of the homes at that time. I thought I could identify those three homes, but there are several new homes in the area now, and I'm just not positive."

The community had expanded with the addition of several new modern homes. The three houses that were present twelve years earlier had all been remodeled and painted and now blended with the new homes. "Jennie, one of these homes has to be the home where the woman lived twelve years ago that we visited with. Hopefully, she still lives here. You remember? The one that gave us some information on the fire and survivors?"

"Yes, I remember, but which house? The houses all look alike, and I'm just not sure which one it is."

"You start over there, and I'll go this way. If either of us gets any positive information, we can call and meet at that location for the details."

Jennie and Andrew each went in opposite directions and began knocking on doors. When the occupants answered, there didn't appear to be any positive responses. Finally, Jennie approached one of the three houses present when the fire occurred and was greeted by an elderly woman. She nodded her head as if to say yes and invited Jennie in.

Jennie thanked the lady and told her she wanted to call her husband and have him present. Jennie called Andrew on her cell phone. "Andrew, I am visiting with Mrs. Adams, and her house was here when the orphanage burned. She may have some information for us."

Andrew joined Jennie and Mrs. Adams. The home was

small but comfortable. The living room contained old and rustic furniture. On the wall were several pictures of individuals, one whom Jenny thought she recognized. "Mrs. Adams, the woman in that picture."

"Why yes, she is my sister; God rest her soul. We lived in this house together for over 20 years."

"Yes, we visited her nearly twelve years ago, and she gave us details on the orphanage fire and indicated that there were a couple of survivors."

"I recall her telling me about a couple she had met. Neither of us was here when the fire occurred. I was out of town for nearly a month and knew nothing about the fire except for what my sister told me."

Andrew went on, "Mrs. Adams, I know it has been twelve years since the fire, but can you tell us anything about the fire or if there were any survivors? We were told that there were none except for a woman who was gone at the time and a thirteen-year-old girl."

"Well, that may not be quite accurate," stated Mrs. Adams. "There were two survivors from the fire, but supposedly a couple of infants were moved two days before the fire. However, that has never been confirmed."

Jennie gasped and looked at Andrew with excitement in her eyes. "Do you remember who the survivors were or anything about the infants? Do you remember if they were boys or girls?" asked Jennie.

Mrs. Adams answered, "One of the survivors was a younger woman, alright, and the child survivor was a thirteen-year-old girl. I have no idea who the two infants were or if it is true that they were even moved. I was gone for several weeks visiting family before the fire and heard about the infants a couple years later."

Jennie asked, "Was the woman Hispanic?"

"No," replied Mrs. Adams. "Why do you ask?"

" I had a very good friend by the name of Maria Cruz who worked there."

"Oh yes, Maria was a beautiful young lady. I miss her so much," replied Mrs. Adams. "She loved all the orphans, and she really loved and cared for a set of twin boys. I was devastated when..." She broke down in tears. After a few moments of silence, she finally continued. "I loved Maria and those twins, and you would have thought that Maria was their mother. I never could understand how the real mother could give up two adorable boys like that." Jennie looked at Andrew with tears in her eyes but remained silent.

Andrew then asked, "Did you know the young woman that survived and where she is now?"

"She didn't exactly survive the fire. The night of the fire, she was out of town. Yes, I knew her, but I didn't care much for her. She was always giving Maria a hard time. I think it had something to do with the twins. She lives across town, and do you want to know something interesting?"

"What is that?" Jennie asked.

"She manages another orphanage. One of two in the area."

"You mean there are two orphanages nearby?" asked Jennie.

"Yes, that's right, two in the same area."

Andrew was quiet for several moments, obviously surprised to hear about the two other orphanages. "How long have the other two facilities been in operation?"

Mrs. Adams thought for a moment and finally responded. "As I recall, both have been in operation for at least fifteen years and maybe even longer."

"Can you give us directions to the orphanage?" asked Jennie. "Oh, and by the way, what is the young woman's name, and do you have any idea how long she has been at the orphanage?"

Mrs. Adams went down the hall into a small room and, after a few moments, returned with a sheet of paper and handed it to Jennie. "Here are the directions to the other orphanage." The young lady's name is Rhonda Dupree. I think she has been there for about seven years. Rhonda has really changed since the fire."

Jennie, looking puzzled, said, "Changed in what way?"

"About four years ago, Rhonda called me and asked if she could pay me a visit. Her call surprised me since we never were very close, but I invited her over. Later that afternoon, Rhonda arrived, and I saw a completely different woman. She threw herself into my arms and started sobbing and begging for forgiveness. She had met a young man who was a Christian, and she herself had accepted Jesus Christ as her Lord and Savior. She and the young man married and now have twin sons."

Jennie jumped up from her chair and exclaimed, "Twin sons!"

"Yes, and I know what you are thinking. Twin sons and a young Hispanic woman who were killed in the fire were the cause of friction between Rhonda and me. Jennie, I think you would like Rhonda, and I encourage you to pay her a visit. Her and I have had several visits since that day, and she has a beautiful family. I will get her number for you. By the way, today is Rhonda's day off, and she is probably at home. They live right next to the orphanage."

Mrs. Adams wrote down the number. Andrew and Jennie thanked Mrs. Adams, said their goodbyes, and left the house.

When in the car, Jennie said to Andrew, "What a wonderful and sincere lady and what a story. A great example of forgiveness and God's grace."

"Yes, it was, but perhaps now comes the hard part. We were silent about Mick and Jake with Mrs. Adams, but I think it might be best to explain to Rhonda our reason for our visit, that is, if she will see us."

"Do you think there's a chance she won't?"

"Seems like Mrs. Adams and this Rhonda have established a close relationship. I think Rhonda will see us, and I think she will also answer any questions we have about the fire and our sons. Only one way to find out, and that's to give her a call."

Jennie looked at the number and dialed it. The phone rang several times, and Jennie was about ready to end the call.

"Hello."

"Hello, is this Mrs. Dupree?"

"Yes, this is she."

"Mrs. Dupree, this is Jennie Hilderbrand, and we are just leaving Ruth Adams home. We had a nice chat with her, and she suggested we pay you a visit. She said you might have some information about an orphanage fire that took place about twelve years ago. We can explain the details if you visit with us."

"Certainly," said Rhonda, "Ruth is a dear friend of mine. I am not so sure I can help, but I would be more than happy to visit with you."

"We should be at your house in just a few minutes, according to Mrs. Adams' directions."

"I will be expecting you soon."

Jennie ended the call, and both her hands were shaking.

"Calm down," said Andrew. "You're shaking like a leaf."

"Oh, Andrew, I just don't know what to expect. How will she react when we tell her the whole story? And what exactly do we tell her?"

"We must tell her the truth. The twins were a result of an unplanned pregnancy and what our intentions were. We don't need to share our whole family history."

Jennie bowed her head, "Dear Lord, give us wisdom in this visit. Help us to say the right thing."

Andrew and Jennie arrived at Rhonda's home. They sat in the car and looked at one another. Andrew squeezed Jennie's hand. They both noticed the orphanage that was adjacent to Rhonda's home. The sign on the orphanage read, "The Good Shepherd's Orphanage." Andrew and Jennie exited their car and approached the front door. They rang the doorbell. Rhonda almost immediately opened it. Jennie introduced herself and Andrew to Rhonda.

"Pleased to meet both of you. Won't you please come in?"

"Thank you," Jennie and Andrew said in unison. They entered the home and noticed several pictures of two boys.

"These must be your twins," exclaimed Jennie. "Mrs. Adams told us you had two lovely boys."

Smiling, Rhonda answered, "Yes, these are our sons. They are a handful, but we love them so much."

Andrew asked, "How old are they, and what are their names?"

"Their names are Jay and Mike, and they are eight years old."

Andrew and Jennie glanced at one another in surprise.

Jennie gasped. "I can't believe it; twins, their names; it is amazing how the Lord works. We will explain in a bit."

"You indicated on the phone that you were wondering about

the orphanage fire that occurred twelve years ago. I wasn't at the orphanage the night of the fire, but perhaps I can answer some questions you might have," Rhonda suggested.

Jennie continued, "Rhonda, this is going to be very difficult for me—I mean us—and we have a confession to make. Mrs. Adams informed us that you worked at the orphanage and that you had some problems with Maria Lopez and her bond with a set of twins."

Rhonda answered, "Mrs. Adams was right, and I guess I really didn't realize it at the time, and I have since apologized to Ruth. I have asked both her and God for forgiveness. Maria was a wonderful woman, and the real reason for my problem was sheer jealousy. She treated those twins like they belonged to her. She paid very little attention to the other children in the orphanage and was very possessive of the twins. She wouldn't even let me hold one. I knew when I eventually was married, I really wanted to have twins, and God answered my many prayers."

Jennie replied, "You have been richly blessed."

"Yes, we have. I am so grateful but also undeserving, especially with my attitude twelve years ago. I'm sorry to have rambled on, but I just had to get that out in the open. I felt so bad, and because of Maria's love for those boys, I chose their name for ours."

"We are both glad you did," remarked Jennie. "It makes it a bit easier to tell you why we are here today. As I said, this won't be easy." Jennie looked very intently at Andrew and nodded at him. Her eyes were filled with tears. Andrew got the hint and proceeded with their story.

"Mrs. Dupree."

Rhonda answered, "Call me Rhonda."

"All right," Andrew went on. "Jennie and I are the parents of Mick and Jake."

Rhonda looked at Jennie and then back at Andrew. Rhonda, astonished, exclaimed, "Oh my, I'm so sorry. "

Andrew continued, "I won't go into a lot of family details, but the twins were born out of wedlock. Jennie knew Maria and knew she worked at the orphanage. It was the perfect arrangement. Because at the time of Jennie's pregnancy, she was working on a project at the marine lab a short distance from the orphanage."

"Yes, I know of that facility. We take the boys there often to view the different sea life specimens. The boys love to watch the starfish and other critters on display."

"We instructed Maria to keep us well informed, which she did. After placing the twins in the orphanage under Maria's care, Jennie and I married with the hopes of keeping the whole affair a secret. We then planned on adopting the twins."

Jennie went on, "After several days, the calls from Maria stopped. We drove from home to the orphanage and discovered it had burned to the ground. We did some checking with the local newspapers and read the details of the fire and the lives that were lost. Needless to say, we were devastated. Talk about forgiveness. We have asked for God's forgiveness many times."

Rhonda asked, "Do you have any children now?"

Jennie answered, "After the birth of the twins, the doctor informed me that I may not be able to have another child. Perhaps this was God's punishment for my sin."

"You know, Jennie, God works wonders in many ways. Don't give up," encouraged Rhonda.

"Thanks, Rhonda. God does work wonders," Jennie

remarked.

"There is another big reason for our being here today," Andrew explained. "There have been some very interesting coincidences that occurred the past few weeks that we can't explain, and we thought we needed to have another look into the fire incident. Can you remember or tell us anything about the fire that might give us some hope that the twins may still be alive?"

"Mrs. Adams indicated that a couple of infants may have been moved prior to the fire. Do you know anything about that?" said Jennie.

Rhonda answered, "I have heard those rumors, but there was never any evidence that young infant twins were ever placed in this orphanage or the other one in this area. There are some things that occurred at the orphanage that I have never told anyone about. I have prayed about it but never felt like God gave me an answer. Perhaps now He is giving me that answer. This may take a bit. Can I get you both something to drink, a soda, water, or something?"

They both said that water would be good, so Rhonda went into the kitchen and filled glasses with ice and water and then returned with the filled glasses on a tray.

Rhonda went on. "I left the orphanage two days before the fire. I told the manager I needed to go home and attend to my parents, but that was not true. I wanted to go to the authorities and report some safety issues I had at the orphanage. Maria knew about those issues as well. Maria told me she was going to write to let some individuals know about some concerns she had with the orphanage and the safety of the twins. She was even thinking about moving the twins. We had been experiencing some terrible electrical storms just before the fire. Of course, these storms are fairly common that time of year.”

“Hmm, we never received a letter, and the storms could certainly explain the reason for no phone calls,” said Jennie questioningly.

Andrew asked, “Were the twins moved?”

“I don’t know. The orphanage burned the night before I returned.”

Jennie asked, “You currently manage the orphanage next door? How long have you been there?”

“I have worked there for six years. Shortly after the fire, I got married, and we had our family. I didn’t want to work while the boys were so young. I love children, and when the position became available, I jumped at it since it was so convenient.”

Andrew asked, “Have you by any chance looked at any of the past records of children that have come or gone?”

“Yes, I have, but there were no indications twins had been taken in. There was a single infant that was placed at about five to seven weeks old; however, this age was questionable. That same infant, a boy, ran away from the orphanage at age eight. The records were unclear on the child’s name. The authorities were notified, but the runaway was never found.”

Andrew and Jennie gasped and looked at one another. Andrew rubbed his jaw and appeared to be in deep concentration. Obviously, Rhonda’s remark about the runaway was troubling him. *Where did that child go?* he asked himself. He stood up and walked over to look at the pictures of the twins. He then walked over and looked out the window at the orphanage next door.

“Rhonda, Mrs. Adams indicated that there were two orphanages in the area,” Andrew stated. “Is that correct?”

“Yes, that is correct. The other facility is quite a bit older than the one next door. I don't know much about it other than it is a much larger orphanage, and it is very difficult to place a child there. They always seem to be filled and have no openings."

"Where is it located?" Andrew asked.

"It is about fifteen miles from here on a large acreage just off Locust Road."

Jennie asked, "Is it rather odd that there would be three orphanages so close together?"

Rhonda replied, "Yes, it is, and I have asked that same question. I did some checking and found out that the original owners or company owned the one that burned as well as the one next door. They no longer have any interest in the one next door, and the current owners are really neat Christians and a real blessing to this area."

"Rhonda, Jennie and I want to thank you for seeing us today on such short notice. You have been a great help."

Rhonda replied, "Could you answer a question for me before you leave?"

Andrew and Jennie looked at each other with concern. Andrew answered, "Sure, if we can."

Rhonda stated, "I have been watching both of you during our visit, and I get the feeling that there is something you aren't telling me, something about the twins. Both of you gasped when I said that a boy ran away a few years ago. Are you thinking…"

Andrew interrupted. "Let's just say that we have had some very interesting things happen recently that we can't explain. Perhaps you have given us some renewed hope."

Jennie asked, "Is there anything else you can tell us about the boy?"

"No, I'm sorry. This all happened before I came. I will do some checking and ask at the orphanage."

"Will you call us if you find out any information?" asked Jennie.

"I will, and I will also be praying for you and Andrew. As I said before, God does work wonders and sometimes in mysterious ways."

Jennie added, "Thank you very much, and yes, He does."

Rhonda gave Jennie a big hug, and tears welled up in her eyes.

"I almost forgot, here's a number that you can reach us," added Jennie. Jennie wrote down a phone number on a sheet of notepad paper that she had in her purse and gave it to Rhonda.

Rhonda said, "Please let me know, well, you know what I mean."

Jennie let her know that she would. Jennie picked up the picture of the twins sitting on a table by the door and stared at it for several moments before remarking, "You have a beautiful family."

The three said their goodbyes, and Andrew and Jennie departed from Rhonda's house and got back in their car. The two reflected on their discussion with Rhonda.

"Andrew, Rhonda seemed very sincere. I also think we may have captured her interest."

"I think we did too, and I also think she will do some more digging on the runaway. At least, I hope she does. As she said, 'The Lord moves in mysterious ways. Jennie, I asked myself something a while ago when Rhonda said that a child ran away at the age of eight. At that young age, where would he go, and just how did he get there? Beaumont is over 300 miles from here. It just doesn't make any sense. If that runaway turns out to be one of our boys, God certainly put a hedge of protection around him. Also, Beaumont is a small community. Why haven't we seen the boy?"

"Oh, Andrew, I just think something positive is going to come out of this."

Andrew added, "We have one more stop before we head home. We are going to pay a visit to the orphanage Rhonda told us about. Didn't she say the location was on Locust Rd?"

"Yes, I believe that it was."

Andrew turned the car to the right off the main road and onto the shoulder and turned off the engine. "Oh, my, we should have gotten directions. I'll put Locust Road in my cell GPS." He put Locust Road into his GPS and studied the coordinates. "Here it is. Locust Road. What road are we on now?"

Jennie looked at a cross sign. "We are currently on Fairview Blvd."

Andrew answered, "Let's see, Fairview Blvd. This will be easy. Locust Road only goes right off Fairview." Andrew and Jennie continued on Fairview.

"There's Locust Road," pointed out Jennie, "Praise the Lord, your cell was right on."

"You sound like you don't trust a cell phone GPS."

"No, Andrew, I don't."

Andrew responded, "You ever tried using one? You have one on your cell phone, you know."

"I know, I just…"

"You just don't know how to use it. Come on, be honest; you don't, do you?"

"OK, you got me." Jennie giggled.

"Well, there it is," replied Andrew.

They pulled over to a pullout and viewed the sign that identified the orphanage. Several children of all ages were seen running and playing, accompanied by a couple of adults. All the buildings on the premises were neatly painted white and trimmed in blue.

"Locust Heights Orphanage. It's huge, and the grounds and landscaping are beautiful," remarked Jennie.

"Yes, it is lovely. I think I see the office sign. That's a good place for a start."

They pulled into the parking area and observed more children playing on swings and slides. A couple boys were playing catch, and some girls were playing with jump ropes. Andrew and Jennie got out of the car and went to the door that had a sign that read, "Office Administrator, Visitors Welcome."

They entered the office. A middle-aged woman rose from her desk and greeted them. "May I help you?" she asked.

Andrew spoke up, "Yes, we have some questions about the orphanage and wondered if by any chance you have any twins in the orphanage that have been placed for adoption? Oh, I'm sorry, this is my wife, Jennie, and I am Andrew Hilderbrand." Andrew removed his wallet and showed the woman his identification.

"Please to meet you," spoke the woman. "My name is Velma Sturgeon. Are you looking to adopt twins? We do have a set of twins."

Andrew and Jennie looked hopefully at each other.

"We currently have twin girls that are seven years of age," Velma informed them.

"Oh, I see; we were actually wondering if you might have a set of twin boys that might be eleven to thirteen years of age?" Andrew informed her.

"No, we have several boys here, but we have never had twin

boys at our facility."

"I understand, Miss, or is it Mrs. Sturgeon?" asked Andrew.

"Miss," stated Velma.

Andrew went on. "Miss Sturgeon, we are not really here to adopt, but we do have some questions regarding a male placement that may have been placed here approximately twelve years ago."

"I see," said Velma. "In that case, I will have to refer you to Mrs. Susan Dolan, who is our operations manager. Her office is in the south wing of the building. I will ring her."

Velma went into another room to make the call. She then returned to inform Andrew and Jennie. "Susan will meet with you. I will show you to her office."

All three left Velma's office, went outside, and proceeded down a concrete walkway to another wing of the complex. Several young children stared at the three. Some of them said hi to Velma. An older gentleman was trimming a large hedgerow. He, too, smiled and said hi to the three as they passed by.

The three entered another wing of the complex, and Velma led to a door with a sign reading, "Operations Manager, Susan Dolan." Velma opened the office door, and they entered. Velma then went on to make the introductions. "Susan, I would like you to meet Mr. and Mrs. Hilderbrand. They have some questions for you. I will leave you three. I have several files to update back in my office."

"Thanks, Velma," Susan said.

Velma left the office.

"Mr. and Mrs. Hilderbrand, I'm pleased to meet you. I am Susan Dolan."

"Likewise. I am Andrew, and this is my wife, Jennie."

Jennie said, "Pleased to meet you also, and thank you for

seeing us on such short notice."

"No problem. You caught me on a day when I am caught up, and there are no pressing issues. Velma indicated you have some questions about our orphanage and perhaps about a male placement that may have occurred about twelve years ago? She also stated you asked about twin boys."

Andrew glanced around the office and noted the wall pictures. He walked over to the office window. He then unbuttoned the top button on his shirt.

"It is very warm today," Susan remarked. "Let me open the window and get some air moving." She walked over and opened the window. "Never have we had twin boys, just girls."

"Yes, Mrs. Dolan, that's what Miss Sturgeon told us."

Susan responded, "Call me Susan. Regarding a male placement twelve years ago, the orphanage has had many male placements since that time and, of course, of all ages. I would have to check our records, and that may take quite some time."

"Yes, we understand. Susan, about twelve years ago, an orphanage burned, and all the occupants except two were lost in that fire, we have been told."

Susan, with a depressed look, replied, "Yes, I am familiar with the fire. I lost a very dear friend that worked there. In fact, I was offered a position there, but I wasn't ready for an orphanage career. I finally was offered this position about four years ago and decided the time was right for me."

Jennie and Andrew glanced at each other with disappointment.

"What field were you in before you took this position?" Jennie asked.

Susan responded, "Actually, I worked at an adoption agency and did counseling."

"Getting back to the fire," Andrew went on, "Jennie and I were very close to a set of twin boys that were reportedly killed in that fire and were close to adoption."

"Oh, I'm so sorry," replied Susan.

Andrew noticed a younger woman employee gardening just outside the open office window. Her attention became focused on the conversation inside.

"The woman we just visited with at the Good Shepherds Orphanage indicated that a young boy about age seven or eight ran away from the orphanage, but he was never located. Were you aware of that?"

"No, I wasn't aware of that, and fortunately, since I've worked here, we have never had a runaway from the orphanage. I don't believe there was ever one prior to my arrival. At least our past records have no mention of one. Our orphanage has always had an impeccable record for caring for our children and making sure children are adopted by respectable clients."

"I'm sure you do, and this is a lovely facility, but we are exploring every possible avenue hoping that some information might have been overlooked at the other area orphanages," responded Andrew. "Jennie and I want to thank you for taking the time to see us. If you find or hear anything about the runaway child from the other orphanage, please contact us. Here are our numbers that you can contact us with. It would be best to call me on my cell at 320-440-5555." Andrew gave the other numbers to the woman on a sheet of paper.

The young Hispanic lady working outside made a mental note of the number and repeated it to herself. She then used her finger to imprint the number in the garden soil. After imprinting the number, she repeated it over and over to herself, not wanting to forget it.

Andrew and Jennie left the orphanage and entered their car. As they were traveling, Jennie commented, "I guess the only thing we can do now is pray for a miracle. We have covered all the orphanages."

"I'm not giving up hope just yet, Jennie. After all, there was a runaway from the other facility. Even though we have covered every location where we live, we still need to check out the big houses on the other side of town and keep rechecking the bike paths and everywhere we had contact with those two boys. It's not that big a town. Those boys can't just disappear."

Andrew's cell phone rang, and he answered it. "Hello."

"Hello, this is Rita. I have some information for you."

"Who are you?" asked Andrew. "Where are you?"

Rita responded, "The orphanage. You were there a few minutes ago."

"Yes, we were there," responded Andrew.

Rita went on., "A short distance from the orphanage is a shady turnout with a picnic table. Can you meet me there? Please come quickly." Rita ran from the orphanage on a path through the woods to the turnout and table.

Rita was a young Hispanic woman and was obviously quite frightened. She kept looking back to assure herself she was not being followed. She also knew in her own mind that what she was about to disclose had to be done. She also knew her job was in jeopardy but still, the voice within kept repeating, *You have to do it, you have to do it. Please, Lord, help me through this.*

"Andrew, who was that?"

"The woman said her name was Rita. Evidently, she saw us at the orphanage and wants to meet us at a picnic table just down from the orphanage. She sounded very frightened and wanted us to get there immediately."

Andrew turned the car around, sped back to the orphanage, and spotted the turnout. A young woman was sitting by the table. Andrew pulled over and parked the car. He and Jennie both got out of the vehicle and approached the woman.

"Are you Rita?" Andrew asked.

Rita replied, "Si, Señor, I am Rita. I work at the orphanage, and I heard you talking to Miss Dolan. Before she came to the orphanage, there was a boy that ran away. He was seven years old. The man in charge doctored the records and told us never to tell anyone. That man is no longer at the orphanage, and I'm glad. None of us liked him very much."

Andrew looked at Jennie. They turned aside, talking softly so that Rita could not hear them. "Jennie, Rita is very frightened and nervous. Let's just listen."

Andrew turned back to Rita. "Why are you telling us this?"

"I have been carrying this burden for many years, and when I heard you talking at the orphanage, something inside…" Rita broke down in tears and started sobbing. Jennie went over to Rita and wrapped her arms around Rita's shoulders.

"There, there, don't cry," Jennie tried to console her. "You can share with us."

"I'm sorry, I loved that boy. He was three years old when I came to the orphanage."

Andrew asked Rita, "What was the boy's name?"

Rita replied, "I never knew his last name. I'm not sure any of us did, but we all called him Jay."

Andrew and Jennie looked at one another, and both had a look of shock on their faces. Andrew asked, "Can you tell us anything else about Jay?"

"He was the smartest boy I have ever seen for his age, even smarter than children much older. He loved to play tricks on other kids at the orphanage. One time, he fooled with the pipe organ in the chapel, and it made very funny sounds."

Andrew and Jennie again looked at one another, grinning.

Rita continued, "That was little Jay's and my secret. No one else ever knew who the culprit was, but Jay told me. We both laughed and laughed."

"Did Jay have any other features, birthmarks, or anything that was different?" asked Andrew.

Rita replied, "I must be getting back. I don't want to lose my job, but the only other thing that was strange is Jay was never seen around other kids without at least a T-shirt on, even on very hot days. Even when we took all the kids swimming, Jay never removed his T-shirt. Something else; not only was he smarter than all the other kids, but he also loved to correct their grammar. I always wondered how such a young boy could be so smart. I prayed and prayed that some nice people would come to the orphanage and adopt *little* Jay. I even thought about adopting him myself, but as a single parent, I knew I couldn't afford to. Then one morning, I went to work, and little Jay was missing, and I cried and cried."

"Oh, dear God, Andrew could it be, could it be our son?"

"I don't know, but it sure sounds promising," answered Andrew. "We have some detective work to do when we get home."

"Please don't tell anyone at the orphanage that you talked to me," said Rita, "I would lose my job, and this is all I know."

"We won't, Rita; you don't know how much help you have been," Andrew told her. "With this information, you have given us new hope. Someday, we will tell you the whole story. By the way, how would you like to double your present salary?"

"Señor, I have no real education. I only know children. My

love is for children and caring for them."

Andrew explained, "I have just the position for you and will be calling you after I work out the details."

Rita answered, "Gracias, I will pray about this, but I really do love working with children. Please, I must go now. I have to get back."

Rita turned and started walking rapidly back on the path to the orphanage. Just before disappearing from sight, she turned and waved vigorously to the couple that now had renewed hope of perhaps both sons still being alive.

Jennie and Andrew got in the car and started toward home. Andrew exclaimed, "This has been a long day but a day that has certainly given us hope. Now we have a long drive home."

Jennie answered, "Yes, we do, and before I fall asleep, what do you have up your sleeve?"

"What do you mean?" Andrew answered.

"What kind of a position do you have in mind for Rita?"

"Just a brainstorm; I need to put some more thought to it. Rest assured, I will come up with something," Andrew stated.

Jennie replied, "I'm sure you will. I could see your wheels turning from the moment you asked Rita about a doubled salary amount. Aren't you tired?"

"I'm wide awake, and I think better when I'm driving. Lean back and get some sleep."

Andrew hadn't driven very far and looked over at Jennie, who was already sound asleep. Andrew reached over, patted her on the shoulder, and smiled.

They continued toward home, and Andrew, deep in thought, clenched his fist and smiled broadly. Silently to himself, Andrew said, "Yes, yes, I've got the perfect position for Rita."

The drive home seemed to go much faster than before and

had given Andrew time to reflect on the day's events as well as his plan for Rita. He rehashed in his mind all the events that had happened with the two boys and the renewed hope that both sons may still be alive.

****

*A*ndrew pulled into their driveway and hit the release button on the garage door. He reached over and gave Jennie a nudge on the shoulder. "Honey, Jennie, wake up; we're home."

"We are already?"

"Yes, and I think I have the perfect solution for Rita. I will fill you in tomorrow morning. Now let's get some sleep. I'm beat."

CHAPTER THIRTEEN

The next morning, Andrew was in the kitchen preparing breakfast. Awakened to the aroma of hotcakes, bacon, and eggs, Jennie entered in her robe.

"Good morning, babe. Did you sleep well?" asked Andrew.

"Wonderful, and breakfast smells so good. I love it when you rise early and fix a nice breakfast. I'm starving."

"It's almost ready. Coffee will only be another minute." Andrew dished up the breakfast, and they consumed it as they were engaged in conversation.

"Well, wonder boy, what did you come up with? Any bright ideas for Rita?"

Andrew, with a smug look on his face, answered, "As a matter of fact, I did come up with an idea that I think just might work. Remember, the church has been toying with the idea of hiring a full-time nursery attendant and helper for the daycare center."

Jennie replied, "Andrew, that's a great idea. Our daycare center and nursery have really increased in numbers with all the new families in the church. We saw all those youngsters at the orphanage that Rita worked with. Rita would be perfect, and she loves working with children. Can the church afford such a position, and you did say her salary would be doubled?"

"Yes, I did," replied Andrew, "And you let me take care of that. I will talk to the Board and lay the idea in front of them. Just remember, Grandpa is a strong supporter of the church."

"Andrew, you devil you!" Jennie and Andrew broke into laughter.

"Not a good choice of words, Jennie. I will talk to CJ and Sara as soon as they get back from Wisconsin. He will be back for the church board meeting, which is scheduled for the Sunday after his return."

"That soon?"

"Yes, the sooner, the better."

***

On a Friday morning two days after CJ returned, Andrew and he met for coffee at CJ's favorite coffee shop. Andrew filled him in on his proposal for Rita, and, just as Andrew had anticipated, CJ agreed that Rita would certainly be a good candidate for the position. Andrew had previously discussed how he and Jennie had met Rita and her enthusiasm for children. Andrew and CJ agreed that it would be best for CJ to call for the special church board meeting on the upcoming Sunday right after church.

***

Early Saturday morning, the couple had just finished breakfast. Andrew had opened his Bible in preparation for his morning devotions. Jennie had receded to her favorite spot as well to do her devotion and Bible reading. Andrew had just opened his Bible to the book of Hebrews and read verse 11:1: *Faith shows the reality of what we hope for; it is the evidence of things we cannot see.*

Then the phone rang. "Now, who could that be at this time of the morning?"

"Hello," answered Andrew.

"Mr. Hilderbrand, this is Rhonda from the orphanage, and we spoke a few days ago. I'm sorry to call this early and on a Saturday morning, but I have discovered some information I think you should know about."

"Yes, I remember our conversation, and no, don't be sorry; how are you?"

"I'm fine, thank you. Since our visit, I have done some checking and found out something that might shed some light on the runaway."

"Yes, go on," insisted Andrew, now in suspense.

"I found out there used to be a trucking firm between the two orphanages. It shut down about three years ago. Evidently, they were caught hauling illegals into the country. Anyway, I asked around and found out that several runaways and other troubled teens in the area used to hitch rides and get off only the Lord knows where."

"Rhonda, do you know that for sure?"

"Yes, I got this information from a number of reliable sources. Anyway, I thought I should let you know. By the way, any sign of those two boys?"

"No, not yet. We have scoured this whole town and all locations where we have encountered the two but still no sign of the boys. Rhonda, thank you so much. You have been very helpful. God bless you, and we will inform you if either of the two boys shows up."

Jennie, still in her robe, entered the room just as Andrew was hanging up the phone. Andrew didn't notice Jennie's entrance and was in deep concentration. "Andrew, what's wrong? Who was on the phone?"

Andrew didn't answer but remained silent. He was considering the information Rhonda had just supplied.

"Andrew, are you ok?"

"Yes, I'm fine. That was Rhonda, the woman at the orphanage."

"Rhonda! What did she have to say? Oh Andrew, hurry, tell me."

"Rhonda said there used to be a trucking firm near the orphanage that was caught transporting illegals and runaways. "

"Dear God, you don't think…"

Andrew interrupted, "I don't know, but it could explain if the boys are our sons, how they got here."

"Hmm, Andrew, didn't both those boys say they lived in big houses across town?"

"Yes, they did. Are we thinking the same thing? Maybe those boys *are* living together. Now wouldn't that be a coincidence?"

Jennie remained silent for a few moments and finally responded, "Yes, it certainly would be."

***

*S*unday morning, the church was packed, and of course, Andrew was looking forward to putting the proposal for Rita in front of the church Deacon and Elder Board. The church choir finished their opening hymn, and the minister entered the pulpit. Jay and Mick were in the top balcony looking down at all the attendees.

"Pst, pst, Mick, look," Jay prodded.

Mick quietly said, "What, look at what?"

"That couple down there, the man and woman in the next to the last row; I've seen him before."

"Yeah, me too," said Mick. "The baseball coach, that is the guy I pitched for."

"I also ran him over with my bike in the park," countered Jay.

"Boy, that lady sure is pretty," Mick commented.

"She sure is," replied Jay.

"I've seen her someplace before." Mick rubbed his chin and was in deep thought. "Hmm, yes, that's it. She's the chick I ran into with my bike in the park. She sure was nice."

"What!!! You ran her over with your bike? That means we each ran those two over with our bikes. We better keep our distance and not let them see us here. I have seen her here before. I think she comes here a lot and always with that coach. They're probably hitched."

Mick said, "Yeah, there's lots of people in this church, and we aren't exactly regular attendees, but at least we're here more than Christmas and Easter people."

"Yeah, you're right. Hey Mick, I've got an idea. Let's follow them after church. We can follow on our bikes. If they get into one car and go to the same house, I bet they are hitched."

"Yeah, good idea. Come on, let's sneak out the back and wait for them. We don't want them to see us."

Jay and Mick snuck down the back steps and exited the church to their bikes. They could see the main church entrance from their hiding location. The congregation started exiting the church.

Inside the church, Andrew was speaking with some men.

He waved to Jennie and pointed to himself and the men he was standing by. Jennie nodded in agreement. Andrew and the men entered a side room while Jennie continued mingling with several women outside the church.

In the church office, nine men and three women were sitting around an oval table. CJ was one of the men and had requested the meeting. Andrew explained to the church board the reason for calling the meeting. He filled the board in on how he happened to meet Rita but did not fill the group in on the details and circumstances of how he had met her. Only CJ knew the details. He knew that, God willing, all the details would hopefully surface in the near future, but for now, he would remain silent.

After several minutes of discussion and questions by various members in attendance, Andrew spoke up, "Well, that about sums it up."

One of the men said, "Well, Andrew, from what you have told us, this Rita sounds like just the person we would be looking for." The man looked around the table at the others. "Any questions?"

One of the women piped in. "If this woman is like what Andrew says, loves children, and has had the experience indicated, I say yes. If both Andrew and CJ feel comfortable, that's good enough for me."

One of the men asked Andrew to contact Rita and see if she would be interested. "If she wants the job, tell her she's hired and salary is not an issue."

"Thank you all," replied Andrew. "I assure you that you won't be disappointed. Let's close in prayer."

***

The boys were in a good hiding spot and watching the people exit the church. "The chick came out, but I haven't seen the guy come out yet," said Jay.

"Me neither; must be havin' 'fession in there."

"You dummy, Mick, it's confession."

"I knew that."

"You didn't either."

The boys continued debating the issue of confession. The fact that Jay liked to correct Mick had always been a point of contention ever since the two had met. Correct grammar usage was one of Jay's strongest attributes and, for a boy of twelve, was remarkable, especially without any formal education. Just how did he get so smart? Mick, on the other hand, although quite smart, was not as polished as Jay, especially when it came to proper dialogue.

Andrew and the others exited the church. "There she is, Mick, and here comes the guy."

"I see them."

***

Andrew and Jenny met, entered their car, and pulled out of the parking lot.

"Well, Andrew, how did the board meeting go?"

"Just as I expected. I was asked to contact Rita and give her the job description and let her know she could have the position. Salary would not be an issue."

"Oh, Andrew, that's wonderful. I just hope she accepts the position."

"You know something? I believe she will."

"Did you tell Sara that we would be a few minutes late for

lunch?"

Jennie responded, "I did."

As the couple drove off, Mick and Jay followed them on the bike path, pedaling as fast as they could. Jay yelled so that Mick could hear him. "We are going to lose them."

Mick replied, "The road turns right up ahead. Come on, we can shortcut through the park."

Mick and Jay took the shortcut and were able to keep the car in view. Andrew stopped at the light, enabling Jay and Mick to catch up but not be seen. Andrew turned right at the next intersection, where a sign read, "Dead end."

"They turned right," Jay reported.

"I seen them, Jay."

Again, Jay's grammatical prowess showed forth. "No, you saw them, not seen them."

"Seen, saw, whatever. Since when did you start teaching grammar?"

Jay went on, "That highway dead-ends in about a mile or two. By the way, you really should polish up your grammar a bit."

Mick replied, "Yeah, I know; keep your eyes open for their car."

"Mick, there it is!"

The car was parked in CJ's driveway. Jay and Mick rode their bikes to a group of trees across from the Hilderbrand home. "Boy, that's a nice house. Now we know where the couple lives," remarked Jay.

"Yes, we do, and we'd better get back to Mr. Croft's house."

Jay and Mick got on their bikes and returned to the church, went down the steps, and entered the house they were living in. The custodian was sitting in a rocking chair, reading his Bible.

Jay asked, "Mr. Croft, you know a lot of people in this church, don't you?"

"Well, yes, I do, nearly everyone in fact."

"Do you know who drives a blue BMW?"

Mr. Croft answered, "There are a couple of people in the church who drive blue BMWs."

"How about a guy that's younger and goes with a good-looking chick?"

Mr. Croft chuckled. "That would be the Hildebrands, and that good-looking chick, I mean, woman is Jennie Hilderbrand, and the guy, as you say, is Andrew, her husband. They are a nice couple, and their grandfather is very wealthy and really supports this church. In fact, he really supports this town."

Jay muttered, "I see."

Mr. Croft was curious. "Why do you ask?"

Jay responded, "Just wondering. They sure have a nice house. It's really in a neat location with all those trees in the back. No houses close by either."

"No, Jay, the house you described is not Andrews and Jennie's. That house belongs to CJ and Sara Hilderbrand, their grandparents."

Mick interrupted, "Come on, Jay, let's go check out the park for cans."

"Yes, let's go. We haven't done that for a while. Should be some."

Mick and Jay went for a ride through the park and stopped at a park bench. Both boys were in T-shirts and cutoffs, sitting in the shade and discussing the morning's activities. Of course, they were eyeing several cute girls walking through the park, only natural for two twelve-year-old boys. Girl watching was much more rewarding than their can collection. Neither of the two was successful with collecting cans. Unlike most can collection days, today was not to be, and neither of them found any.

Mick commented, "Someone must have gotten here ahead of us."

"Looks that way. At least there are some pretty girls out. Whew, it's hot today."

"It sure is. Glad we wore these cutoffs."

"You know, Mick, I read a funny story yesterday, well, not so funny, but interesting."

"What about?"

"Well, there were these two sixteen-year-old brothers who were pretty competitive and were always betting each other who was the most daring."

"So, what happened?"

"The two decided to look around and locate a house that looked like a good candidate for their caper."

"So, what was the caper?"

"They made a deal that one would enter the house and take something out, and the other one would put it back."

"Isn't that stealing?"

"Well, hmm, not exactly, more like borrowing."

"Well, did they pull it off?"

"Yup, and never got caught."

"Was anybody home?" questioned Mick.

"Nope."

Mick had a sarcastic expression and responded, "Why, shoot, that would be easy. I could do it with the owners at home and in bed."

"Yeah, I bet you could. You know you couldn't do it."

"Could too, and I'll prove it. You pick the house."

"OK, I will, and I know just the house."

"Yeah, and where is it?"

"The one where we followed the couple to. They are old people and probably can't hear very well. They probably go to bed early, too."

"That's a good idea, and the coach and his wife wouldn't know either, not that it matters. Since it is kinda stealing, we'll have to repeat of our sins. You know stealing is a sin."

"Yes, I know it is, and also dummy, it's *repent*, not *repeat*."

"I knew that," confessed Mick.

"Yeah, seems like you always know that. Come on, let's cruise over there and have another look at that house."

The two boys climbed on their bikes and went to check out the outside surroundings of the elder Hilderbrand home. The house appeared to be a two-story house with a basement and was surrounded by a chain-link fence and many older shrubs. There were no other houses in the immediate area which would lend themselves to the planned caper. No neighbor eyes watching the house would make it much easier. In the back of the house was a large, wooded lot where the boys could make a quick getaway if needed.

"You know, Mick, since you think you are so good, I'll take something out, and you put it back."

"Deal, just take something small."

"I will, maybe a picture or knick-knack of some kind."

"Sounds good; just make sure the owner will know it's missing."

"Yeah, I know that's what makes it exciting. If we pull off this caper, the old couple will tell the young couple, and the story will spread like wildfire. We will even be one up on the couple I read about because no one was at home when they did it."

"Yea, that's cool. We may even be heroes."

The boys got on their bikes, rode in opposite directions, and resumed their search for pop cans. After an unsuccessful search, the boys rode back to Mr. Croft's house.

CHAPTER FOURTEEN

The church had announced a movie night. Mr. Croft had told the boys he would be attending. He invited the boys, but they weren't much interested in the movie that would be showing. This was the night the boys had decided to initiate their caper, and this movie night at the church would work out perfectly.

"Hey boys, sure you don't want to see the movie?" asked Mr. Croft. There will be soft drinks and popcorn."

"Nah, I think we will just hang out," replied Mick.

"OK, but it will be late when I get home. See you in the morning then."

"Hope you like the movie," Jay hollered as Mr. Croft left.

The boys had a little discussion on what had just happened. "Mick, I think we just told Mr. Croft a little white lie."

"What do you mean?"

"You told Mr. Croft we would just hang out."

"Yea, but we didn't say where."

"Yea, you're right; let's get going."

They arrived at the large house after dark and noticed that the house was in complete darkness. However, there was a streetlight that lit up a portion of the front lawn.

"Mick, the house is totally dark. I bet the old couple is at the movie."

"Perfect," replied Mick.

The boys hid their bikes near the wooded area behind the house. The night was deathly quiet except for an occasional hoot from a night owl emanating from the woods. The boys approached the dark house with caution but with confidence, their escapade would be successful.

"Sure glad Mr. Croft wasn't home tonight. We would have had it difficult explaining going out together after dark. Doesn't appear that anyone is home here tonight either, which should make it easy, that is, if I can find a way to get in."

Mick responded, "Yeah, I'll have the exciting part."

Mick and Jay started circling the house in search of an entry by checking the side door and all the ground-level windows. Jay neared the back of the house and found a door that was unlocked. Jay exclaimed, "Here we go; you stay here. This won't take long and should be easy."

Jay removed a small mag light from his pocket and entered the unlocked door. He turned on his light and entered through a second door leading to a large kitchen area. Shining the light around the kitchen area didn't reveal anything that Jay felt was suitable to his liking. He then entered a massive living room. Although lavishly furnished with several antique pieces of furniture, nothing caught his eye. Jay then passed through the living room into a hallway. He shined the mag light onto a wall across from CJ's office.

Pay dirt.

In the middle of the wall, at about eye level, was an 8x10 picture of CJ and Mickey Mantle. "Ah, perfect," whispered Jay.

Jay removed the picture and backtracked to the outside, where Mick was waiting.

"What did you get?" questioned Mick. Jay showed the picture to Mick. "Wow, Mickey Mantle and some other guy. That's a great choice and will be easy to put back."

"That other guy is probably old man Hilderbrand. I wonder if he was a baseball player."

"I don't know, but look, Jay." Mick pointed at a set of car lights turning into the long driveway leading to the house. "They must not have gone to the movie; it wouldn't be over yet."

"No, it wouldn't. Let's get out of here and pronto."

The boys rushed to their bikes and cut through the woods on an old path they had discovered earlier that led to the main road. They rode to the church and set their bikes aside. Jay then went down a set of steps to the church basement, then removed a loose brick and retrieved a key. He unlocked the basement door and passed through the kitchen area to an unused storage room. He then placed the stolen—or what the boys liked to call borrowed—picture behind some old doors leaning against the wall. After replacing the key, Jay commented, "Well, that takes care of my part of the caper. Now smarty, you can put it back."

"I will, but give it a few days to let things quiet down some after they discover it missing."

"That shouldn't take long. The picture was in plain sight on the wall."

"By the way, Jay, where did you get that basement key?"

"I found it down by the basement door and tried it in the door lock, and it worked. That has been my key to success these past few years. Key to success, do you get it?" as Jay laughed at his own cunningness.

"Yes, I get it," replied Mick, disgusted that he did not have a counter-remark.

The next morning, CJ was sitting at his home office desk with the door open, looking at the wall in the hallway. He was a bit puzzled, thinking to himself, *Something is wrong here. Something is missing.* He got up and went over to examine the wall. *That's it; the Mickey Mantle picture is missing.* "Sara, did you move the Mickey Mantle picture?"

Sara was in the kitchen and hollered back to CJ. "Why, no. What's wrong?"

"It's missing, and I haven't touched it."

"Oh, my, has someone taken it?"

"I don't know, but it sure looks that way."

"Look around and see if you can detect any other items missing. I'll look around in here some more."

Both Sara and CJ went through all the rooms carefully and could not detect any other items missing.

CJ even called Andrew, but he hadn't removed the treasured picture. He did ask about its disappearance. "Who on earth would steal a picture of you and Mickey?" asked Andrew.

"I guess we should notify the sheriff," stated CJ. "I think it's also about time to have an alarm system installed, maybe acquire a big guard dog. With no immediate neighbors in the area, I've considered both options for quite a while."

"Oh, CJ, is a guard dog necessary?"

"Times are changing, Sara, and we can't be too careful these days."

"Maybe you're right, but don't get a mean one."

CJ chuckled. "The meaner, the better."

A few evenings later, while Mr. Croft was attending a Bible

study, Jay and Mick were discussing when and how to return the Mickey Mantle picture. Since the removal of the picture, both boys had felt not only uncomfortable about their actions but also guilty. The previous Sunday, the pastor had given a sermon on the Ten Commandments, and of course, *Thou Shalt Not Steal* really jumped out at the boys. The thought of fessing up and just returning the picture had entered their minds, but they decided to follow through with their caper.

"Mick, we better get that picture back into that house. Oh, our deal, you better get it back."

"Yeah, I had alright. First, I need to scout out the house for an easy way to get in. Don't forget they were gone when you took the picture, and a door was unlocked."

"Yeah, I know."

"That door you entered might not be unlocked this time, so I need to scout out the house for another way to get in."

"Yes, I know, and I have been thinking about that a lot. Have you ever thought about what if we can't find a way to get into the house?"

"Not really, it's an old house, and it has a basement. I bet it has a ground window to sneak through."

"Yeah, you're probably right. Let's sneak out early next Sunday and go check the house out in the daylight. There aren't any close-by houses, so nobody should see us. "

"Good idea. How did you decide to take a picture anyway?"

"You saw the picture. Mickey Mantle was a hero and played for the New York Yankees. It probably meant a lot to the old geezer since he was in the picture, too."

"Yeah, you're right. It probably did mean a lot to the old guy."

Sunday morning found the church packed in anticipation

of the announced annual church business meeting. The pastor reminded the congregation, and of course, both boys heard the announcement and were thrilled with the idea of the members being in church longer than usual.

Jay and Mick were in the balcony in their usual spots alone, remaining unnoticed because of their strategic location. As they looked down, they noticed all the Hilderbrands seated next to each other in the pew. Jay pointed out and whispered to Mick. "This is perfect. The business meeting will probably last a long time."

"Yeah, I bet it will. It is a perfect time to leave early and go check out the house."

Jay agreed, and they both left the balcony and exited their usual way out of the church. The exit portal had always been Jay's escape route since living in the church.

The boys mounted their bikes and headed for the Hilderbrand house. Before arriving at the house, the boys did a quick observation of the surroundings and saw nothing that appeared unusual. Mick informed Jay, "We have to be quick and hope the church meeting takes a long time. You go around that way, and I'll take the other direction."

As the boys were departing in opposite directions, they heard a dog growling and barking in the rear of the house.

"Not good," responded Jay. "There wasn't any dog around when I took the picture."

"Just be careful and hope the dog is confined."

The boys continued around the house, and as Mick approached the back gate, he spotted the large, growling Doberman who was shut in a chain-length dog run. Mick talked to the dog. "Easy boy, you are ok." The dog looked at Mick and quit growling. About that time, Jay came from around the house.

"I don't like the looks of that dog; he looks mean."

"Yea, but he quieted down when I talked to him. It will be ok."

"I sure hope you're right. See any way to get in?"

"No, not yet," responded Mick. The boys started back around the house. "Jay, wait a second; look behind that big shrub."

"I see it." Behind the shrub was a 2x3 ground window.

"I'll check it out." Mick went to the window, which was a slider. He pushed on the window to one side, and it opened. "I'm in luck; check this out."

Jay crept up and looked with Mick through the window, which revealed the basement in the house.

Mick stated, "I have an idea, Jay. I'll jimmy the window so it can't be completely shut. I bet the old couple never even looks at this old window, and it is kind of out of sight. It will be easy to get in, but it won't be as easy as you had."

"Yeah, the outside back garage door was unlocked for me."

"We better get going, Jay. That business meeting may be about over."

The boys mounted their bikes and peddled back to the church. Upon arrival, they saw the congregation exiting the church. Mr. Croft was climbing the steps from the church kitchen with several containers of food. He met the boys at the house.

"Here you go, boys," said Mr. Croft. "Say, by the way, my sister and her family want me to visit with them for a few days and will be picking me up in the morning. I will be back on Saturday afternoon. I figure you boys will be ok 'till I get back. You both know my rules, so see to it that you follow 'em. Deal?"

"Deal, and don't worry," Jay and Mick said in unison.

Jay and Mick ate with great gusto.

"Boy, this is good," remarked Jay.

"It sure is. Fried chicken is my favorite, and the potato salad is yummy."

Mr. Croft added, "I'm glad you like it because I brought back quite a bit left over from the business meeting dinner. There was a lot of food left after the meal. Lot of regulars today, but they didn't seem to have the appetite they usually have, so I brought down plenty to last you while I'm gone."

The boys both thanked him.

"Well, I'll leave you, boys. I better put some things together to take with me tomorrow."

Jay responded, "I think Mick and I are going to take our bikes and see how the pop can situation is in the park. We didn't have any luck the last time."

"You boys are amazing, mowing lawns, picking up pop cans," commented Mr. Croft. "What are you doing with all your money?"

"I don't know about Mick, but I am saving mine," responded Jay.

"Got something you want to buy, huh?"

Jay answered, "Nope, college."

Mr. Croft was surprised and remained silent a few moments. "College? What about high school?"

Jay replied, "I'll take a college entry test. I bet I can do better than most high school kids."

Grinning, Mr. Croft answered, "Well, Jay, knowing you, I just bet you can. What about you, Mick?"

Mick looked at Jay with a devilish grin on his face. "I think college, too. Anything Jay can do, I can probably do better."

Jay said, "Cannot."

Mick countered, "Can too."

Mr. Croft interjected, "Now, now boys, I'm sure you both will do just fine."

"Come on, Mick, we better go make some money."

Jay and Mick left Mr. Crofts, picked up their bikes and sacks, and headed for the bike path in the park. When they arrived at the park, Jay, the organizer that he was, organized the route each would take. He suggested that they take the routes they had used before and then meet at the bench afterward as usual. Mick agreed with that. Both boys took off in opposite directions, both stopping several times to pick up pop cans. They arrived at the park bench, laid their bikes down, and sat on the bench. Both boys' sacks were full of pop cans. Mick noted that it looked like they both had done well today, and Jay agreed.

Pop can collection had paid good dividends to both boys for several years. Only recently, since becoming friends, did they take their cans in for exchange at the same location. At five cents a can, the rewards had mounted up substantially for both boys. Unlike other twelve-year-old youths, neither Jay nor Mick had spent their money on unnecessary items but rather had chosen to accumulate and save for what they hoped would lead to a college education. Both had periodically exchanged their coins for paper money and kept it in a safe hiding place not disclosed to anyone. Very seldom was the paper money counted in fear of revealing their hiding locations. The fact that both had also kept their lawnmowing money had resulted in a very sizable amount, and other arrangements were going to have to be made in the very near future.

After a bit of discussion about their trips around the park, Mick said to Jay, "You know, Mr. Croft will be gone this week.

I think it's time for me to keep up my end of the deal and return that picture. I know how to get into that house, and it will be easy."

Jay agreed. "How about tomorrow night?"

"OK," Mick replied. "We'll go over about 9 p.m. and wait till the lights are all out and they are in bed. They're old, so they'll probably be asleep by that time."

Jay responded, "Yep, let's get these cans home and put them with the rest of our collection."

"Let's take the cans in tomorrow for collection. We're running out of storage space for them." The can collection was being stored in a small shed behind the Croft home. It would take several trips to the recycling site.

"Sounds good to me."

The boys picked up their bikes and bags of pop cans and headed across the park to Mr. Croft's house. The afternoon before the night of their big caper, the boys went over their plans. They discussed all the possibilities, including a successful picture put-back and what if they got caught. Both had become a bit anxious, but a deal was a deal, and, of course, Mick was positive he could pull it off. He also knew that performing his end of the caper would put him one-up on Jay. Since becoming friends, the two had become very competitive in almost everything they did. Mick had seemed a bit more daring, but Jay was a step ahead in head knowledge. How this would play out in the future and God's will for these two was yet to be determined.

CHAPTER FIFTEEN

The night of the big picture put-back had finally arrived. The boys felt like they had covered all the details. Their biggest concern was the guard dog in the back of the house.

"Mick, what will you do if that dog starts barking? That could ruin our plans."

"The window I jimmied is on the side of the house. The dog is in the back. I didn't see any sign of a doghouse, and it was confined behind a chain-linked fence. Bet they keep the dog in the house or in the garage."

"I sure hope so. That was one mean-looking dog and big, too."

"I think it was a Doberman."

"You wait here, and I'll get the picture." Jay went down the steps to the unused janitor room and removed the picture from its hiding spot. After replacing the key behind the loose brick and locking the basement door, he joined Mick at the top of the stairs.

"Got it," stated Jay. "Let's go."

***

*A*fter arriving at the Hilderbrand home, the boys placed their bikes in a spot for a fast getaway. Unfortunately, there were several lights on in the house.

"Hope they aren't night owls. Wonder what time it is?" Mick asked.

"I think it was 9 p.m. when we left Mr. Croft's house."

"Must be close to 9:30 by now."

One by one, the lights went out inside the house. "Look, the lights are out," Mick noticed. "I hope they are sound sleepers."

Jay replied, "Better wait a while until they get to sleep. Wonder if we should have waited until we knew they were gone?"

"Naw, this will make it more challenging. Anyway, they were gone when you took it. I'll be up on you when I return it while they are home." Mick had made a point of letting Jay know he would be one-up on him on several occasions. "It goes on the wall across from an office, right?" asked Mick.

Jay replied, "Yes, and there were two smaller pictures on each side that were also baseball players. Don't worry about where it goes. Just put it anywhere where they will see it."

Before approaching the entry site behind the shrub, Mick remarked, "Wait, Jay, I want to sneak around the back to check if the dog is outside." Mick quietly circled the house and returned. "No sign of the dog."

"Is that good or bad?" questioned Jay.

"It's good. The dog is probably in its kennel in the garage, sound asleep."

"OK, and you're probably right," responded Jay.

The boys went behind the tall shrub, carrying the picture. Mick tried the sliding window and easily opened it.

"Jay, hand me the mag light."

Jay handed Mick the light and held the picture while Mick crawled through the window.

"Give me the picture. This will only take a couple minutes."

Jay handed Mick the picture.

"Don't make any noises as you go up the stairs. The old couple won't hear you, but I'm nervous about that dog."

"Why do you think I wore my sneakers?" replied Mick.

Mick set his feet on the floor and shined the light around to get his bearings. He spotted the stairway that led upstairs. He looked around and slowly started ascending the stairs. He reached the first floor and cautiously started down the hall with the picture in hand. He did not see a revolving camera mounted to a spot on the ceiling that was recording every move he made. Mick set the picture on a table across from CJ's office.

A red light started blinking and beeping on a wall panel in CJ and Sara's room. "Sara, look!" CJ exclaimed.

"What, what's wrong?" responded Sara.

"Someone is downstairs!" CJ's answered. Sara looked at the red flashing light and heard the beeping.

"Oh my!!" she cried. CJ hopped out of bed with pajamas and donned a robe.

"Sara, call 911 and tell them to get someone here fast. Tell them our alarm went off and we think a burglar is in the house. I will let Buster out of the pantry. Give me a minute and turn on the alarm! The outside lights will go on automatically." CJ turned a stair light on and started down the steps. He reached the pantry and let Buster outside.

Just how good a guard dog Buster was, CJ had no idea. This was going to be the first test for the big dog. But from reports, CJ had heard that the Doberman breed had an excellent reputation for being very effective in not only scaring the living daylights out of any intruder and, given a chance, putting the intruder in his place. CJ had been told that just the bark and vicious growl had stopped many would-be perpetrators. This dog had been professionally trained not to bite or maim but to knock down and hold an individual by a pant leg or shirt sleeve. CJ was about to see just how good this professionally trained dog would perform.

Mick saw the lights on and ran toward the stairs leading to the basement. He heard the alarm go off. As Mick neared the lower step, he fell but quickly got up and made his way toward the exit window. Mick crawled through the window, where Jay was nervously pacing. Jay looked around and saw the dog running towards them from the back of the house. Mick also saw CJ approaching them. "Let's get out of here!" Jay shouted.

Both boys started running toward their bikes. They almost reached their bikes when the big Doberman pounced on Mick, knocking him down. Buster grabbed Mick's shirt and held on with a vicious growl. The shirt sleeve ripped, revealing a birthmark under his armpit. The dog stood over Mick. Jay saw the mark and stopped immediately, mouth open wide in disbelief.

Mick said to Jay, "Get going!"

Jay didn't move but continued to stare at the birthmark under Mick's arm. A patrol car pulled into the driveway with red lights flashing and a loud siren blaring. CJ reached the boys and looked them both over. He saw the birthmark on Mick's arm and remembered what Andrew and Jennie had described.

The two patrol officers approached. "What do we have here, CJ?" asked one of the officers.

CJ responded, "Well, Jack, what we have here is perhaps a miracle and an answer to prayer." The officers looked at one another and shook their heads in disbelief.

CJ looked at Jay and motioned for him to come and stand by him. Jay complied. "Son, I want you to remove your shirt for me."

Jay slowly removed his T-shirt. A birthmark was revealed at almost the identical spot as Mick's. Jay looked away from CJ and focused on Mick. Mick looked up at Jay and saw the birthmark but remained silent as though his tongue was tied.

"Just as I suspected," responded CJ.

"Will we go to jail, mister?" asked Mick.

"Boys, you will both be going to a much better place," promised CJ. "Buster, release!" The big Doberman immediately released his stronghold on Mick's shirt. "Are you okay, son?"

"I think so," stuttered Mick.

CJ checked Mick over to make sure Buster hadn't broken the skin on Mick's arm. "OK, son, you can stand up."

Mick was visibly shaken, as was Jay, who had not uttered a word since all the action began.

"Just a minute, boys, and we'll go into the house. Jack, you and Skeeter can go back to your dispatch, and by the way, you got here pretty fast. I'm proud of you two, and I'll put in a good word for both of you. Makes me feel a lot better about our local police force."

The patrolmen got in their cars and drove away. They began conversing about the incident as they left.

"Now, what was that all about?" asked Skeeter.

"I have no idea. Looked like a burglary or at least an attempted one. Old CJ can be a bit strange at times, but I'm not going to question him. It sure will be interesting to talk to him later and get some details, though. Those two lads were scared to death, and I can't say I blame them, especially the one the dog had under control. That was one mean-looking dog. Wonder where and when CJ acquired him?"

"I don't know," responded Jack. "However, I bet those boys will remember this night for a long time. Yes, I bet they will. Skeeter, did you recognize either one of those boys?"

"No, come to think of it, I didn't. Neither one was very old. Why on earth would they happen to pick CJ's house to attempt a burglary?"

"I have no idea."

***

CJ led the boys into the house where Sara was waiting. "What on earth is going on? Who are these boys? Why does this poor lad have his shirt ripped off him? Did Buster do that?"

"Sara, I know it's late, but call Andrew and Jennie. Tell them to get over here immediately."

Sara went over to the phone and dialed the number. The phone rang several times, and finally, there was an answer.

"Hello," answered Andrew, half awake.

"Andrew, I'm sorry to be calling you at this late hour, but CJ insisted. Please hurry. He wants you and Jenny to get over here immediately. CJ said to tell you that you will be shocked when you see who is standing in our living room."

Andrew responded, "Is something wrong? Are you two all right?"

Sara replied, "We have had some excitement, but… you will see when you get here."

"Hurry!!" CJ responded loud enough for Andrew to hear.

"I'll wake Jennie, and we will be there in a jiffy."

Jennie entered the living room and asked Andrew if that was CJ. Andrew responded, "No, Sara, Jennie, get dressed and hurry. We need to get over there and pronto! Sara sounded hysterical, and I'm afraid something terrible has happened."

Jennie and Andrew hurriedly dressed and drove to the Hilderbrands. On their way, Jennie again questioned Andrew, "Did Sara give any indication of what was wrong?"

"No, just for us to get there pronto."

They arrived at the home and rushed to the door, and rang the doorbell. Sara, visibly shaken, opened the door, and they entered the house. CJ and the boys were standing in the room, and both boys had robes on that were way too big for them.

CJ started out, "Jennie, Andrew, I want you to meet a couple of boys who apparently like pictures of ballplayers."

Jay and Mick looked at one another with very sheepish looks.

Jennie, with excitement in her voice, said, "Andrew, it's the boy on the bike!"

Andrew responded, "Yes, and the one that knocked me over, too. These are the baseball pitchers I told you about."

CJ and Sara looked at one another with smiles. CJ then regarded Andrew and Jennie. "Well, you two, I now want you to see something that I'm sure will interest you. Boys, take off your robes." Both boys slowly removed their robes and now stood in their jeans only. They both stared at Andrew and Jennie and then down at their feet, obviously embarrassed. They both raised their arms, revealing their identical birthmarks.

"Dear God, our sons," Jennie said as she started to sob. "Andrew, our boys, it's our boys!"

Andrew, with tears of joy in his eyes, responded, "Yes, thank you, Father. You have answered our prayers."

Jay looked at Mick with surprise. "What, sons? You mean Mick and I are brothers?"

Jennie replied, "Yes, yes, and I'm your mother, and that's your father." Jennie and Andrew gathered the boys in their arms one at a time and embraced each of them.

"But how could we be brothers? We both ran away from an orphanage," Jay said questioningly.

Jennie replied in tears, "We know and, oh, Jake, Mick, we are so sorry. You are so young, but we pray that you will understand after hearing the whole story."

CJ approached the group. "Boys, I'm CJ, and that is Sara, and we are your great grandparents."

Jay and Mick looked at CJ and Sara and then at one another, smiling. "Hey Jay, remember the first day we met in the big house?"

Jay replied, "You mean church?"

Jennie and Andrew could no longer maintain their composure, and both broke out in tears, tears of joy. After a moment, Jennie, somewhat composed, finally asked, "You boys met in church?"

"Yes, we both lived in different churches. They both had good food after the preacher was done."

All the Hilderbrands broke out in laughter.

Mick voluntarily proceeded. "We don't live in a church anymore. We live with the janitor who lives by the church."

"What's his name, Jay?"

"Mr. Croft."

All four grownups were completely surprised and shouted out in unison, "Mr. Croft!!"

"That's our church," Jennie said in dismay.

"Yes, we know that. We have seen you there several times from the balcony," stated Mick.

"From the balcony!" exclaimed Jennie. "You mean you boys

have been in church all these Sundays watching and listening from the balcony?"

"Yes," replied Mick.

"That's amazing."

"Which one of you two lived in the church by Mr. Croft?"

"I did," responded Jay, "And snuck food to eat."

"Mick, you can show us tomorrow which church you stayed in," Jennie asked.

CJ glanced at the wall clock, noting that it was after midnight. He suggested, "Andrew, we could stay here all night and learn a lot more about our lives, but you and Jennie should get these boys home and get more acquainted. There will be a lot of catching up to do later."

Sara agreed. "Yes, and CJ and I want to hear all about it. Isn't God good!"

Jennie, Andrew, and CJ all said together, "He sure is!"

"Andrew, you, Jennie, and the boys come over tomorrow for a celebration dinner and tell us all about it. The boys can pick up their bikes then."

"Good idea, what time?" Jennie asked.

"Oh, around 5 p.m. would be great," CJ responded.

"Sounds good," said Jennie. "We will talk to the boys and see what their favorite food and, of course, favorite desserts are. Is that ok with you boys?"

Both boys agreed and had big smiles on their faces.

Sara chipped in, "Jennie, you call me early and let me know what the menu is."

All the adults and the boys huddled in the living room, and CJ gave a prayer. After the prayer had ended, the boys responded with a hearty, "Amen." All four adults looked at one another with obvious surprise on their faces.

Andrew, Jennie, and the boys left the house, entered their vehicle, and started for home. The conversation on their way home was nonstop—so much to talk about, so many questions that needed answers. They arrived home, and Jay and Mick were in awe at what they saw.

"Wow," said Jay, "Is this where you live?"

"Well, yes, Jay, but from now on, this is where we all live," responded Andrew. They all exited the car and entered the house.

"Jake, umm, I mean Jay," began Jennie.

Jay replied, "That's ok; was my real name Jake?"

"Yes, it was, but you know what? I like Jay even better, and from now on, Jay it is," replied Jennie.

"Great," replied Jay.

"How about you, Mick? You okay with Mick?" Jennie asked.

Mick replied, "Yep."

Andrew entered the room holding a couple of T-shirts. "Boys, you can use these to sleep in tonight. Tomorrow we will all go clothes shopping."

Jay and Mick looked at one another with big smiles. "I have never gotten to buy new clothes," responded Jay.

"Neither have I," seconded Mick.

"Well, everyone, it has been a long and exciting day and evening, I might add, but it's now 1:00 a.m., and I suggest we all get some sleep. We all have a lot more to talk about tomorrow," said Jennie.

Andrew agreed and asked the boys to come along, and he would show them to their rooms. Jennie wished the boys good night, and the boys told her the same.

After getting the twins to bed, Andrew and Jennie retired to their room. Although it was after 1 a.m., both were wide awake and much too excited to think about getting to sleep.

They both prayed and thanked God for uniting them with their sons. Both agreed that it would take some time to acclimate as a family. They sensed the birthmarks would be a very sensitive issue and would approach that issue with caution. Andrew would again check with doctors for advice on the necessary treatments for port-wine birthmark removal.

After viewing the marks on the boys that evening, neither of the boy's birthmarks had shown any evidence of enlarging. However, their age might perhaps cause some problems that would require alternative removal methodology. It was undoubtedly a situation that would have to be discussed with the boys. The fact that both boys had identical marks that now had been revealed to four people might ease the tension that the marks had created. Andrew would also ease the tension by explaining to the boys that he had had the same birthmark and in the same location, another coincidence, and it had been successfully removed.

They would deal with the birthmark issue later, but for now, the Hildebrands had been blessed with the reuniting of their sons.

"Jennie, do you realize that little episode the boys had tonight at CJ and Sara's might well have been a blessing."

"What do you mean?"

"If CJ hadn't caught them, who knows when or if we would have found them."

"Yes, I guess I hadn't realized that. God certainly had a plan. He turned a bad experience by our twins into a good experience for all of us."

"Kind of a Joseph and his brothers experience, like in the Bible, wasn't it?"

Finally, after 2 a.m. and much more discussion, Andrew and Jennie turned out their night lamp. Jennie, however, had one more closing remark. "God is so good, and we need to give Him all the glory. We sinned, but God has forgiven us and has answered our prayers by giving us back our precious boys."

CHAPTER SIXTEEN

On Saturday morning, both Hilderbrand households were bursting with excitement. Sara and CJ were reflecting on the previous evening's excitement. Sara could hardly contain herself wanting to call Jennie, but CJ had to calm her down, letting her know it was only 6 a.m. and the younger Hilderbrands were most likely still in bed. He, of course, had to inform Sara that Buster, the newly acquired guard dog, had performed quite admirably and done exactly what he had hoped for. Sara offered her comments as well, stating, "Those boys were frightened to death, especially the one Buster had pinned to the ground."

"You know Sara after the boys get to know us better and spend some time around here, Buster and those boys will be the best of friends."

"I hope you're right, CJ. I guess I'll wait till 9 a.m. but not one minute later to call Jennie."

"That will work."

***

Jennie was in the kitchen with a smile from ear to ear,

singing to herself as she prepared breakfast. At exactly 9 a.m., the phone rang. Jennie picked up the receiver. "Hello."

"Good morning, Jennie. How are the twins this morning?"

"They're both still sound asleep. I think they were overwhelmed last night. You should have heard them last night on our ride home. They both talked non-stop, and I think I could write a book of their past ten or twelve years." Jennie said.

Sara replied, "We can't wait to hear all about it."

"Sara, there are a few things I want to share with you in private. You can fill CJ in. Those boys have been through a lot, but they both are extremely intelligent and industrious for their age. Neither has had any formal schooling, but get this: they both have been collecting pop cans, mowing lawns, and doing other odd jobs to save money for college. Their money is hidden in Mr. Croft's house and somewhere in the church. Evidently, it's quite a sizable amount."

"Well, bless their hearts."

Jennie went on. "Don't mention the birthmarks; both are very sensitive to those marks. Andrew still thinks they can be removed without difficulty. I think I hear the boys stirring, so I better run. We'll see you later. Oh, by the way, Jay loves pork chops, but Mick likes fried chicken with mashed potatoes and gravy."

Laughingly, Sara answered, "We will have both. What about a dessert?"

"They both also love cherry pie and ice cream."

"That's CJ's favorite, too. See you later then; I better get cracking. I want to make this a special day for the boys."

Jennie heard the boys and Andrew in the living room talking, and she couldn't wait to see them. The talking was quite muffled, but she surmised the boys were excited. After all, neither of the twins had probably gotten to go shopping for clothes in a shopping mall.

"Did you two sleep ok last night?" asked Andrew.

"Yeah," replied Jay.

"What about you, Mick?"

"I did too."

"I bet you boys are hungry."

"I don't know about Jay, but I'm starving."

"Me, too," replied Jay.

"I bet Jennie has breakfast about ready. Let's go check." Andrew and the boys headed to the kitchen, where Jennie was preparing breakfast.

"Good morning, boys; I heard you say you were starving."

"We sure are," replied Jay.

"It will be ready in a jiffy. Go ahead and have a seat."

Andrew and the boys seated themselves, and Jennie sat a platter of ham and eggs on the table accompanied by a platter of hash browns and toast.

"I hope you boys like ham and eggs."

"Do we ever," responded Jay.

"Yes, we're used to eating cold cereal most of the time. Mr. Croft didn't eat a big breakfast like this, just toast and coffee," Mick revealed.

Andrew asked the blessing over the food and told the boys to dig in. The boys exhibited table manners expected from an adult by saying please and thank you. As they ate, there were many discussions and comments, but Andrew and Jennie knew there would be many more during the years ahead, and they were so interested in hearing all that these two were willing to share.

"Boys, after breakfast, we have a big day ahead of us. We are all going shopping. Your mother and I have a few things we need, but most of the day belongs to you two."

Jay said to Mick, "Did you hear that, Mick? We now have a real mother and father."

"Yes, and a real home to live in."

Jennie was in the kitchen cleaning up the breakfast dishes, but she overheard the comments from Jay and Mick. Tears were streaming down her face, and the look on her face was priceless. Andrew was also having a hard time controlling his emotions. After composing herself, Jennie joined the others and admonished, "We better get moving."

They all exited the house, and Andrew backed their BMW out of the garage. This would be the twins' first ride in the BMW, as they had ridden in Jennie's car the night before.

"Wow, Mick, we get to ride in a fancy BMW."

"Yeah, this is really cool. The only transportation we've had is our bikes."

Both Andrew and Jennie broke out in laughter.

Jennie asked, "Have you boys ever gone to a shopping mall for clothes?"

"No, Mick and I have just gone to thrift stores and bought our clothes and shoes. They're cheap, but we don't need anything fancy."

Mick joined in, "Besides, we are trying to save our money."

"You said last night on our way home that you were saving for college."

"Yep," replied Jay.

"I'll tell you what, Andrew and I are going to let you two pick out whatever clothes you want and we are buying. You two keep your hard-earned money."

Of course, Jay and Mick were both all smiles with that

arrangement.

Upon visiting several kids' clothing departments and trying on various outfits, the necessary purchases were made. To Jennie and Andrew's surprise, neither boy went overboard and only purchased a few outfits, and all purchases were very conservative.

After the last purchase, Andrew made a suggestion that met approval with everyone. "I spotted an ice cream parlor outside the last store we were in. How does an ice cream waffle cone sound?"

"Great idea, Andrew," agreed Jennie.

"What's a waffle cone?" questioned Jay. Mick asked the same question.

"You'll see," replied Andrew.

Arriving at the ice cream shop, Andrew ordered four large chocolate waffle cones. After consuming their cones, Jay stated, "Boy, that was tasty; now Mick and I can say we have had waffle cones."

A couple hours after having waffle cones, Jay insisted they stop at Billy's hot dog cart. Jay knew exactly where Billy and his cart would be. Billy was at the stand with several customers.

"I used to get free dogs at this stand," Jay pointed out.

"How did you do that?" asked Andrew.

"I told a lot of people about the good hot dogs that Billy had. They are the best hot dogs ever."

"You know we just had ice cream cones, but a hotdog sounds so good," responded Andrew.

"Yes, it does," seconded Jennie.

The four remained in the car until the customers had left the cart. As they approached the cart with Jay in the lead, Billy exclaimed, "Hey bro, haven't seen you in a while. What's happenin'?"

"A lot, and I want you to meet some people."

"More customers?"

"Well, yes, but more than just customers, I want you to meet my brother Mick and my dad and mom."

"What!! What do you mean brother, dad, and mom?" exclaimed Billy with a look of surprise."

"I'll tell you all about it one of these days over hot dogs."

"I will hold you to that and praise the Lord. I'm so happy for you; four dogs coming up on the house."

Jennie looked at Andrew and rubbed her fingers together, indicating that Andrew would pay for the hot dogs. Andrew got his wallet out and started retrieving the money for payment.

"No," responded Billy. "This young lad has been my best salesman for several years, and four dogs is the least I can do."

Billy prepared four hot dogs with all the fixings and presented the Hillderbrands each with a hot dog. The four sat at a nearby table near the cart and consumed their hot dogs with great gusto. After returning to the car, Andrew remarked, "That was without a doubt the best hot dog I have eaten."

Jay was all smiles when Jennie and Mick agreed.

Andrew continued, "We will come here very often in the future and perhaps make it a part of our weekly activities."

"No 'perhaps' to it, Andrew. Hot dogs will be a weekly occurrence," replied Jennie.

"I agree, and we have got to introduce CJ to these hot dogs. You know how he loves hot dogs."

Mick and Jay were all smiles during this interchange.

"He seemed like a nice young man," remarked Jennie.

"Yeah, he is," replied Jay. "He goes to church, and I think he is a Christian. When I told him I was living in a church, he told me we would have to have a talk someday about Jesus."

Andrew and Jennie looked at each other with big smiles. Jennie asked Jay, "Do you know what church?"

"No, but he told me where it was and what it looked like."

Jay gave a description of the church and an approximate location. Mick was intently listening to Jay's description and burst out, "Hey, that's the church I was staying in."

Again, Andrew glanced at Jennie and just shook his head. "This is absolutely amazing. I can't believe it. Not only is God amazing, but He also has a sense of humor."

Jay and Mick looked at each other with puzzled looks, but neither spoke.

As the four continued their tour, the boys pointed out several nice homes where they had lawnmowing jobs. Jay showed the couple the mission he stayed at before moving his location to the church. As they continued, Mick also pointed out the mission church where he had been staying prior to moving to another larger church where he could remain more anonymous. Mick explained that they had offered meals to needy people after the sermon. Andrew asked why the boys had moved from their initial locations, and both he and Jennie were a bit surprised but also pleased with their responses.

Although living in different locations, both boys had indicated that some of the other boys living there were using bad language and even shoplifting. They both remembered while living in their respective orphanages that these two activities were not acceptable. Both agreed that what they had done at CJ and Sara's house was wrong and would apologize for their actions. After describing the details as to why they had taken the picture and being caught while trying to replace it, Mick asked, "Will Grandpa and Grandma be mad at us?"

Andrew looked at Jennie, who now had obvious tears of joy in her eyes—tears that reflected the words *grandpa* and *grandma* but also the boys' remorse for what they had done. Andrew responded to the boys' concerns. "Boys, your mother and I are so proud of you for your honesty and sharing with us. As for your grandpa and grandma forgiving you, they are both strong Christians, and forgiveness is one of their strong Christian attributes. I know in my own heart they have probably forgotten about your little caper, as you called it. In fact, I kind of think your little episode was rather comical, but of course, I would never tell CJ that. My father has told me many stories involving your grandpa and some of the shenanigans he was involved in. Some of them ranked right up there with yours."

The final stop for the day was the church and the house of Mr. Croft. Mick and Jay got out of the car. Jay was about to enter the Croft house but was surprised when Mick went down the steps to the church basement. "Hey Mick, what are you doing?"

"Come down here, and I will show you."

Jay abruptly turned around and joined Mick at the bottom of the stairs. Jay watched Mick as he retrieved the basement door key from behind the loose brick. Mick proceeded to unlock the door and enter into and through the kitchen to the storage room where Jay had hidden the Mickey Mantle picture. Mick reached behind the old door frames and retrieved his satchel containing his hard-earned money.

"When did you decide to move your money to this hiding spot?" questioned Jay.

"Just a few days ago. I figured it would be safe here and a lot closer than where it was."

"I'm curious; where was it hidden before?"

"I hid it in an old abandoned car body in a thicket a short distance from the last church I lived in."

"Wasn't that kind of risky?"

"Nah, I kept the money in a locked metal box that was chained to the frame underneath the car body."

"Wow, that was good thinking. Well, let's go get our belongings and my money from Mr. Croft's house. I want to show you where my loot has been stashed."

The boys returned the key and went to gather their belongings. The boys entered the house and proceeded to their room. Jay pulled out the bed from the wall and pulled a small woven rug aside, revealing a square area that had been cut out from the floor. Jay lifted the false wooden floor and retrieved his bag of money. "I found this spot when I moved in with Mr. Croft."

"OK, I told you where my old hiding place was. Where was yours?"

"You should know. It was kept in the same spot as you have been using, in the old storage room behind the old door frames."

Jennie and Andrew had remained in the car and were reflecting on the day's events. "Andrew, these boys of ours are amazing, aren't they?"

"They sure are. It's hard to believe that they are only twelve years old. I still remember what Rita said about Jay while at the orphanage. As I recall, she said Jay was much smarter than kids his age and even smarter than older kids. I am beginning to see why. After we tell the whole story to CJ and Sara, I would like to make a suggestion, and I'm sure CJ would approve."

Jennie responded, "Yes, and what might that be?"

"I would like for CJ to talk to our pastor and ask if it would be possible to set aside time after church to tell our story starting from the beginning. The boys wouldn't have to speak. We can do that for them. It would be too much for them."

"Oh, Andrew, that's a wonderful idea. Let's ask CJ tonight."

"I will," Andrew said, "Keep in mind, Jennie, it may be difficult for us also."

"Yes, I know."

The boys finished getting their belongings together, and Jay said to Mick, "Well, I think I have everything of mine." Jay held up a mesh bag with his belongings and a separate bag containing his money.

"Yeah, me too," responded Mick.

"I guess our money was the most important," Jay remarked.

"Yeah, it was. How much do you have?"

"Don't know, haven't counted it lately.

"No, me neither," stated Jay. "We will have Jennie, er, ah, our mom, this might take a while, put it in the bank for us."

"OK, and yes, it may take a while."

"Mr. Croft gets back next Saturday," Jay noted. "I'm going to write a note for him and let him know where we are, let him know that we'll see him Sunday at church."

"Good idea. I bet Mr. Croft will really be surprised when he finds out who our parents are. I bet a lot of the church people will be surprised, too. Well, let's go."

Jay and Mick exited the house, and Jay made sure the door was locked. They entered the car where Jennie and Andrew were anxiously waiting. "Well, boys, did you get all your belongings?" questioned Andrew.

"Yes," Jay answered. "Neither of us had much. The money bag was the most important."

Mick concurred but added, "And our ball gloves."

Andrew looked at Jennie with a big smile.

Upon arriving home, both boys dug through their mesh bags and pulled out separate bags, which they handed to Jennie.

"We would like for you to put this money into a bank for us," requested Jay. "It's for college." Jennie looked at Andrew, and both had a gleam in their eyes.

Jay continued, "We want to keep our lawn mowing jobs if it's alright with you."

Andrew smiled. "If that's what you want."

"Yes, it is," said Mick.

"Fine with us," replied Andrew.

CHAPTER SEVENTEEN

It had been a day of laughter, anxiety, and just being a family, but the upcoming evening was to be a big celebration dinner at CJ and Sara's. Andrew and Jennie were looking forward to sharing with them. Just how the boys would handle the evening with grandparents, they didn't really know.

Jennie looked at her watch. She realized it was almost 5 p.m. and that they had better get ready to head to CJ and Sara's for the big dinner. The boys knew there was going to be a big dinner that evening, and there had been some anxious moments about how they would bond with the elder Hilderbrands in light of their activities a couple of nights earlier. Andrew and Jennie had sensed the boys' concern and assured them that there was nothing to worry about.

The young family arrived at CJ and Sara's and were greeted by CJ. "How are you? Did you have a busy day? I think Sara has dinner ready, pork chops and fried chicken."

Jay and Mick had big smiles on their faces.

"Oh wow, that's our favorite," Jay replied very enthusiastically.

CJ went on, "And cherry pie and ice cream for dessert."

"That's our favorite too," added Mick.

Sara let them all know that dinner was on. They all gathered around the dinner table, and CJ asked the blessing. "Heavenly Father, we are thankful for this day and the many blessings we receive. We are thankful for bringing Jay and Mick home to us and the safety you have provided for them. We thank you for this food and the hands that prepared it for us. In Jesus' name, we pray. Amen."

As they sat down at the table, there was much discussion about the meal and the day's activities. Jennie was surprised how the boys opened up. The dialogue of the boys, especially Jay, was remarkable. Jennie's conclusion was that God had certainly gifted these boys.

After the main dinner, Sara went back into the kitchen to bring out the dessert. Jay and Mick, in unison, said, "Oh wow, yum!!" The adults giggled over the response.

After dinner, they all went back into the living room, and CJ started the conversation. The boys discussed all the activities they could remember over their twelve years, including describing the orphanages where they had lived, the trailers they had ridden in, the boys in the different churches, the odd jobs they had had, and on and on. They were very open about sharing their lives. Sara, having tears in her eyes from hearing their stories, left the room. After a few moments and composing herself, Sara returned to the room to see CJ shaking his head. "Unbelievable, and to think, right under our noses. What a story."

After sharing information about their time at the orphanages, the tension of the boys had subsided; they were much more relaxed. Finally, Andrew asked, "Would you boys like to share with us why you decided to run away from the orphanage? Do you remember any of the people who worked there?"

Jay was the first to respond. "A couple of the boys I liked were picked up by a couple adults on two different occasions. I think the right word is adopted." The four adults looked at one another with astonishment at Jay's knowledge. "After those boys left, the other kids at the orphanage were either a lot younger or much older. One of the older boys told me about a boy he knew that was not in the orphanage but had hitched a ride on a truck and went into a large city. His parents were always quarreling, so he made the decision to leave home. There was a younger lady that I really missed, and I liked her a lot. We used to laugh and joke around with one another. I remember one time I made the organ sound funny, and I told her about it, and she really laughed and told me I was a naughty boy but that she would not tell anyone about it. Her name was Rita. I wonder if she still works there?"

When the name Rita was mentioned, the four grownups looked at each other but didn't let on that they knew who she was. This was going to be a big surprise for both Jay and Rita come Sunday morning.

"Well, Mick, that about sums it up for Jay; can you remember why you decided to leave the orphanage?" asked Andrew.

The forthcoming response by Mick was something that would tear into the hearts of all the Hilderbrands. Mick, usually full of enthusiasm and anxious to volunteer information, suddenly became very selective and refined. "Most of the kids in the orphanage were girls, and most of them older than me. I had a couple of friends that were boys, but they were adopted. I was very jealous of those boys and wondered why no one never came to adopt me. One day at the orphanage, we got to go on a field trip to a farm nearby. On our way, several trucks passed our bus, and I heard one of the workers at our orphanage tell another worker that one of the trucks that passed us was always picking up hitchhikers on their way to nearby towns. They hoped that someday that company would be shut down. I got to thinking that is what I should do since I didn't have any good friends left at the orphanage. I didn't like the manager either. I don't think any of the kids did. A few days later, that's what I decided to do, and I'm glad because now I have a mom and dad."

"Yes, and a grandpa and grandma too," replied Jay.

By this time, there wasn't a dry eye in the room. Jennie was sobbing out of control and collected both boys into her arms. "Mick, Jay, we are so sorry, and this Sunday, Andrew and I will be telling our whole church family what we have done. You two boys will hear the whole story, and I only pray you will understand and forgive us."

Mick looked at Jay, "We will, won't we, Jay?"

"We sure will," replied Jay.

After several moments of reflecting on what the boys had shared, CJ broke the ice with a much lighter topic and conversation. "I understand you two boys are quite the ballplayers. Do you boys know that your father and I and Andrew's dad were all pitchers? Your father's dad was a good one and pitched a few years in the minor leagues."

"Gee, that's cool," responded Jay. "Who did your dad play for?"

"He was in the Yankee organization and played for their triple-A affiliation until he injured his shoulder in a motorcycle accident. It was too bad because I think he was close to being called up to the big leagues. I like to pitch but sure wasn't the pitcher my father was," replied Andrew. "Enough about us;

I want to know where you boys learned to pitch so well. I have only gotten to see you guys in one game, but I saw enough to know that you both have a lot of talent. In fact, Carl and I… you both remember Carl, don't you?"

"Yes, he was the coach I pitched for," replied Jay.

"Well, anyway, he and I have discussed putting together a traveling team to play against teams in other nearby towns. All players would be between twelve and thirteen years old. You boys will both be thirteen come spring, and from what I have seen, you two would most likely be our pitchers. How does that sound?"

"Great, I can hardly wait," exclaimed Mick.

"Me neither," seconded Jay.

"I thought you two would be tickled. Now getting back to my question, where did you two learn to pitch so good?"

Jay jumped in. "I've played in a lot of pickup games but never really been on a team. I used to go out in an open field by a gravel pile and bat rocks for hours. One day I met an older boy that had a catcher's glove, and he and I would play catch a lot. He always wanted to be a catcher, and I wanted to pitch. I was just lucky, I guess, because I could throw strikes and had a good fastball."

"That's an understatement," commented Andrew.

"I never have been on a team either but played with other guys in pickup games. I used to go out to an old shed with a rubber ball and throw it against the door and pretend I was a pitcher. I guess we both just herited it."

"You dummy, Mick, that's inherited it."

"I knew that."

All the Hilderbrands broke out in laughter. CJ ended the baseball conversation with a suggestion. "How would you boys like to see the Yankees play next season?"

"Oh, wow, that would be super," replied the boys in unison.

"Consider it done. We will all go to a game next season, well, at least us guys, when the Yankees come out here to the West Coast."

A car arrived in the driveway. Andrew noticed a woman and a young girl exit the car and start up the walk towards the front door. Andrew asked, "CJ, were you expecting company?"

"No, not that I know of."

The doorbell rang. CJ went to the door and opened it. "Yes, may I help you?"

The woman asked, "Yes, may we come in?"

"By all means," CJ encouraged. The two visitors entered the room.

The woman said, "You don't recognize me, do you?"

"Something inside me tells me I should know you. Sara, come in here." Sara entered the room and walked over to where CJ and the two women were standing. She looked directly at the woman. Sara, in shock, spoke, "Dear God, can this be true?"

The woman answered, "Yes, mother, it's me, I'm Lou Ann, and this is my daughter, Jenny." Sara fainted and fell to the floor. CJ and all in the room gathered around her.

"Give her room; this is quite a shock for her, actually both of us. I'm speechless." CJ took Lou Ann and the daughter into his arms. After a few minutes, Sara came around, and Andrew helped her up. Sara rushed over to CJ, and the new arrivals embraced.

"Dear child, we thought you were…ah…ah…"

"Don't say it, mother; you thought I was dead."

"But we received a letter saying…" Sara started in but was cut off.

Lou Ann cut in. "…that I had taken my own life?"

After a moment of silence, Sara replied, "Yes."

"I was going to, to save you and father so much grief, but God had another plan for me. After I gave birth to Jenny, I accepted Jesus as my Lord and Savior and made the decision to go to the mission field. Jenny and I have been in the Congo the last fifteen years." Lou Ann addressed her daughter. "Jenny, meet your grandpa and grandma."

"Hello, I'm pleased to meet you," Jenny said to her grandparents.

"Jenny, we both are so pleased to meet you, too," Sara replied. "Oh, CJ, isn't God good?"

"He certainly is. He has brought our daughter, our granddaughter, and great-grandsons safely home to us."

"Oh, Lou Ann, your father and I are so happy you have returned. You will stay, won't you?" asked Sara.

Lou Ann answered, "Only for a short while. I will stay to allow some time for the healing process and for us all to get reacquainted. The Lord has a lot of work for us to do in the Congo. We have committed to another four years and, Lord willing, will return stateside to live and dedicate our lives to the Lord's work."

Lou Ann looked at the rest of the family members. "Who are these two handsome lads?" she asked.

CJ responded. "These two handsome lads belong to Andrew and Jennie." He hesitated for a moment. "That's another story. Let's all have a seat and share some real blessings that we have received just recently."

All the family gathered on a large sectional in the living room and began sharing their stories. After a couple hours of sharing, CJ stated, "Well, after that, I think we could all agree that God has truly and richly blessed us."

Andrew broke in, "Hey, Jennie, remember what I suggested a few days ago?'

"I remember, and after today, the story becomes more amazing."

CJ and Sara looked at each other, puzzled. "What have you two been up to?" asked CJ.

Andrew started explaining, "We thought it would be nice to inform our church of all that has happened, and now with Lou Ann and Jenny arriving here this evening, the story becomes even more rewarding."

CJ was thrilled. "Why, Andrew, consider it done. I'm sure the pastor would certainly agree. Lou Ann, are you and Jenny agreeable to sharing your testimony?"

Lou Ann responded by asking her daughter, "Would it be ok with you, Jenny?"

"Yes, that would be fine."

"Would next Sunday be ok, or is it too soon?" CJ asked.

Andrew answered, "Let's go for next Sunday."

They all agreed.

CJ stated, "In light of the miraculous arrival of Lou Ann and Jenny, who I'm sure will have some wonderful stories to share on how the Lord is working in the Congo, I will have the pastor set aside a full day, or however long it takes, to share with us next Sunday."

***

That night after the twins had long since gone to bed, Jennie and Andrew again had one of their late-night conversations. Andrew said, "I know I'm being boastful again, but our boys showed a lot of maturity. I know we hardly know them,

174

but don't you sense perhaps they have some knowledge of the Lord? Maybe they had Sunday School at the orphanages. They both lived in different churches and must have heard some of what the sermons were about. We know that Mr. Croft is very dedicated to the Lord and, knowing him, I bet he has dropped some subtle comments on his Lord and Savior."

Jennie continued. "Andrew, Mick's confession about his reason for leaving the orphanage tore my heart out. God was certainly working in Mick's life as well as ours. Do you realize that if Mick had been adopted, we might have never seen him again? We wouldn't have even known if he was still alive."

"Yes, I was thinking that very same thing. It's a miracle how God has been working in our lives. I, too, was proud of our boys today, and wasn't the arrival of Lou Ann and Jenny a real blessing as well?"

"Yes, it was, and I'm so thankful for CJ and Sara knowing their daughter is alive and well and doing God's work. I can't wait to hear their testimony next Sunday. I think the church family will be in a state of shock when Lou Ann and her daughter are introduced to the congregation."

"You know, Jennie, there may be a lot of surprises in Beaumont Calvary Chapel this week."

"Oh, Andrew, I'm so excited, but I'm also a bit nervous about sharing our story with our church family."

"We just have to pray that the Holy Spirit will guide us in our deliberations and the congregation will understand and forgive us. I have been praying about it, and I think it might be best if we fill Jay and Mick in on some of the details before introducing them to the congregation. We certainly don't want them to feel uncomfortable hearing the whole truth for the first time in front of a lot of people they don't even know."

"I agree, but you know what, after our experiences with those boys so far, I think they will handle the pressure just fine," replied Jennie.

"I do too, and if the boys want to share with the congregation, I think we should let them. You know something else?"

"What?" responded Jennie.

"I think we should let Mr. Croft know what is planned for Sunday. He may or may not want to share, but I think he should be given the opportunity."

CHAPTER EIGHTEEN

The Sunday of planned testimonies came. The church sanctuary was packed with people, including several visitors. An organist was playing in the background. The congregation began to quiet down as the pastor entered the stage behind the pulpit. Behind and to the right of the pulpit were eight high back cushioned chairs.

The pastor began. "Good morning. I want to welcome you all here this morning. This morning I am going to do something different. I am not going to preach a sermon."

There was applause, and one fellow shouted out, "Amen."

This, of course, brought a round of laughter from the congregation. The pastor smiled and looked up. "Well, Lord, how do I respond to that?" The church audience again erupted in laughter. The pastor continued. "This morning, we will be blessed by some miraculous testimonies from some of our members, as well as guests. We will hear some stories on forgiveness that will touch the hearts of many of you out there in the audience. I anticipate a lot of tears will be shed, but after hearing from our speakers, a lot of joy will fill this sanctuary."

CJ had arranged with the pastor and Andrew to have the

twins, Lou Ann, and her daughter kept in a side room in the back of the church out of sight until the congregation had been seated.

There was a lot of concern and anticipation on the faces of many of the attendees as they looked around. The Pastor continued. "CJ Hildebrand, a member of this church, approached me this week and told me an amazing story. I asked CJ if his family would be willing to share their story with the church members and guests this Sunday. CJ spoke with his family members, and they have consented to share their amazing stories. The service may last longer than normal, but I assure you that you won't mind at all. CJ has arranged for a catered grand buffet after the service in the fellowship hall. Everyone is invited to stay. Feel free to visit with the family as well. I'm sure many of you will have questions. OK, I think it's time to call CJ up, and he will introduce his family members."

CJ walked up to the pulpit, cleared his throat, and looked at the congregation. "God is good, isn't He? Thanks, Pastor. At this time, I would like to call up my family members. I will call up family members you all know first. Sara, Andrew, Jennie, come on up." The three walked up and stood by CJ on his right. "Now, I want to introduce some family members you don't know."

There was a stir, including whispers and soft conversation throughout the sanctuary.

"Lou Ann and Jenny, come on up." Lou Ann and Jenny approached CJ from the rear of the church and stood on his left. The members of the congregation looked around at each other with surprise, and the soft talk became much louder. "Lou Ann is our daughter, and Jenny is our granddaughter, whom we have never seen."

A buzz was circulated around the congregation. Many had looks of shock, and mouths were wide open. Several of the ladies were reaching for tissues.

"A number of you sitting in this sanctuary today perhaps knew Lou Ann when she was a teenager and have wondered whatever happened to her. Sara and I had no idea that Lou Ann was alive and certainly wasn't aware of her daughter. Lou Ann will tell her story a little later." CJ got a bit choked up and motioned Andrew to approach the pulpit. "Andrew, I want you or Jennie to call up the final family members."

The congregation sat in complete silence; many looked alarmed and were stunned in disbelief. They looked to the back of the church.

Andrew and Jennie walked to the pulpit. Jennie had tears in her eyes. Jennie whispered, "Andrew, you will have to do this."

Andrew took the mic. "At this time, Jennie and I would like our sons, Mick and Jay, to come up to the front and join us." Mick and Jay, dressed in suits and ties, walked slowly to the front of the church. They both smiled but maintained their composure. As they approached the pulpit, the congregation was stunned. Many of the ladies had tears in their eyes. Jennie and Andrew were standing hand-in-hand, and both had big smiles. The boys mounted the steps and stood between Andrew and Jennie.

Andrew asked, "Which one first?"

Mick approached the pulpit. "Hello, my name is Mick Hilderbrand, and I am twelve years old." Mick handed the mic to Andrew.

Andrew continued, "Next."

Jay approached the podium. "Hi, my name is Jay Hildebrand, and I am twelve years old."

A petite Hispanic woman cried out from the back of the church, "Oh, dear God, Hallelujah!" after Jay introduced himself.

A member of the congregation stood up and shouted in a loud voice, "Hey, that boy mows my lawn."

Another lady across the sanctuary also stood up and hollered out, "That other boy mows my lawn."

A third older lady, the one that had increased Jay's pay, boldly stood up and shouted, "He does a wonderful job, too."

CJ took the mic from Andrew and remarked, "My, my, it looks like several of you folks already know these boys."

The congregation stood up in unison and applauded. Many shouted out, "Praise the Lord!" Smiles and hugs were plentiful throughout the congregation.

Andrew continued. "CJ, there is one more individual that I would like to call up to the front. Without her being brave, these boys may not be standing here today. Would Rita Sanchez please come up?"

Rita, the Hispanic woman who made the outburst just moments earlier, stood up and ran to the front and up the steps. She rushed to Jay and hugged him hard with tears streaming down her face. Jay looked a bit puzzled but also looked as if he recognized Rita.

"Dear God, thank you, thank you. I know this boy, the orphanage. Don't you remember me, Jay?"

Jay said a bit hesitantly, "Yes, I think I do. We were friends. Now I remember. We played tricks at the orphanage."

Rita answered, "Yes, yes, we did."

Andrew and Jennie began laughing. Andrew then approached the pulpit and gathered Rita and Jay in his arms. He then motioned them to their seats.

Andrew began. "Well, folks, this sermon—I mean these testimonies—may take a lot longer than two hours. Some of you know who Rita is and the relationship she has with our young kids. What you just saw is a testimony of how Rita is on fire for the Lord. Well, CJ. I guess I should proceed."

CJ, with a big smile, approached the pulpit and took the mic from Andrew. He looked at the clock on the back wall of the church. He stated, "Well, folks, it is already half past the hour, and we really haven't begun with our stories. With the pastor's permission, I suggest we sing some old hymns and break for our meal. If any of you need to leave or have other plans after church, feel free to leave. I would like a show of hands of those who feel they need to leave so I can inform the caterers how much food to bring."

Not one individual raised a hand. One parishioner stood up and shouted, "Take all afternoon! I wouldn't miss this for anything!" Many in the congregation shouted, "Amen." The congregation all stood and began to sing some old hymns. Rather arranged by CJ or the hand of God, the first hymn chosen was "When the Roll Is Called Up Yonder." This hymn just happened to be Jay's favorite song. To all the Hilderbrands' surprise, Jay was right at home and sang out the words when the pianist began playing the tune. The Hilderbrands all looked at each other with big smiles matching those throughout the congregation. After several more hymns, the members of the congregation moved into the fellowship hall.

***

The caterers hadn't arrived with the food yet, but no one even noticed. All the family members, including Lou Ann, young Jenny, and the twins, were mobbed by church members.

Hugs, tears, and joyous conversations were evident throughout the fellowship hall. This indeed was a joyful moment at the Beaumont Calvary Church, but the afternoon to follow would be one that would never be forgotten.

The caterers arrived with the food, which was set up on a double line of tables, allowing for buffet-style serving. After the meal, the congregation members left the fellowship hall and went back into the sanctuary. The pastor approached the pulpit and looked out at the congregation. "My, my, are my eyes playing tricks on me, or are there more people here this afternoon than before lunch?" the pastor asked.

Laughter came from all over the congregation. There were indeed more people in the church. In fact, the balcony, normally empty, was now full. It was obvious that many had phoned friends to let them know what was coming that afternoon. Since the Hilderbands were well-known in the community, people just naturally wanted to hear the testimonies and meet the new family members. "Would CJ and your family please return up front here? I'm sure we are all excited to hear how God has been working in your lives."

All the Hilderbrand family members returned to the stage and took their seats. CJ remained standing and approached the pulpit.

CJ called Andrew. "Andrew, I would like for you and Jennie to share with us first. I know both of you are nervous, but trust me, the Holy Spirit will guide you and give both of you strength to get through this."

Andrew and Jennie rose from their seats and approached the pulpit. Both appeared a bit nervous as CJ handed the mic to Andrew.

"Thanks, CJ. Brothers and sisters, today, Jennie and I want

to share with you our testimony of how God has worked in our lives these past twelve years but mostly these last few months. Neither of us are very thrilled of what we have done and can only beg for your forgiveness."

The church was deathly quiet, and all eyes were focused on Andrew and Jennie. Andrew began, but Jennie moved forward, took the mic from Andrew, and whispered, "Andrew, I have to go first."

"Are you sure?"

"Yes, I have to do this." Before continuing, Jennie bowed her head and quietly whispered a prayer. "Father, help me through this."

Jennie looked out at the congregation and began her testimony. She started from the beginning with her pregnancy and the details of her project at the marine lab. She explained in detail her relationship with Maria at the orphanage and the resulting fire that had taken the lives of all the occupants, which they had assumed included their sons. She disclosed that the doctor at the orphanage had informed her she may never be able to give birth to additional children. She left nothing out. Upon completing her story, she handed the mic to Andrew. As before, one could have heard a pin drop.

Andrew proceeded in giving the details of his and Jennie's coincidental meetings with the boys in the park and how both boys had run away from different orphanages and lived in different churches. He also told how Rita was so instrumental in uniting family members. Near ending his story, Andrew looked at the boys, and to his surprise, both boys nodded.

Jay approached Andrew and took the mic. He was composed as he began his comments. "I have lived in the basement of this church for some time. You really have good food after the sermons, which I had heard while hidden in the balcony." Giggles erupted after this comment.

Mick continued next. "I used to live in a shelter but moved to a church across town. A man next to the church caught me one day and asked me to stay with him. He had to move to Oregon and asked me to go, but I wanted to stay. I then tried this church and met Jay, who was staying with Mr. Croft next door.

Mr. Croft stood up and approached the front of the church. "These two boys are probably the best-mannered boys I have ever known. Of course, I can't condone their sneaking and hiding in the church. I suspect a few of you men in the church today have all done little things that probably were as bad, or worse, than what these two have done. I know I sure have. They are very industrious boys, too, collecting and selling pop cans and mowing lawns. These boys would make any parents proud. Praise God for uniting them with Andrew and Jennie. I feel like I've lost family. I will miss having them around and hearing their grammatical spats with one another. I'm sorry for keeping this a secret. We made a deal not to tell anyone, and the boys kept their end until just recently. I pray that this church family will forgive me." Mr. Croft then left the stage.

"Thank you, Mr. Croft, for your kind remarks. You will be seeing them in church on Sundays, and if the boys want, you can join them for the after Sunday meal." Andrew then continued. "Well, that's our story, and we both should have known better and ask now for your forgiveness. Isn't it amazing how God works in our lives? Jennie and I certainly are not proud of how this story unfolded, but, praise God, we are truly blessed and overjoyed with how it has ended. CJ, I guess you need to take it from here."

CJ approached the pulpit, and Andrew handed him the mic. CJ then wiped his teary eyes and cleared his throat. "I'm so proud of these two. I know it took a lot of courage to share their story with you, but isn't it wonderful how the Lord has worked in their lives and brought this lovely family together? Lou Ann, would you and Jenny please join me at the pulpit?"

Lou Ann and her daughter approached the pulpit.

"Lou Ann is our prodigal daughter that has just returned," stated CJ. "Lou Ann has shared with us since arriving Saturday evening, and we are so proud of her and our granddaughter." CJ handed the mic to Lou Ann and said, "Go ahead with your testimony, and by all means, please share why you left home years ago. It is something that Sara and I will always regret, but it needs to be included."

Lou Ann took the mic and began her testimony. "I want to thank you for letting me give my testimony here this afternoon. We have just heard some testimonies on how our Lord and Savior has worked in the lives of members of the Hilderbrand family. I, too, made a terrible mistake early in life and made the decision to leave home and not cause CJ and Sara more heartaches after losing their oldest son and my brother in the war. Of course, I knew about the will but won't go into details at this time. After delivering Jenny out of wedlock, I did a lot of praying and accepted Jesus as my Lord and Savior. I heard through the church I was attending that the Congo was reaching out and in need of missionaries to share the gospel. I made the decision to step out in faith and go there."

Lou Ann went on to share what God had been doing in her life in the Congo. Many lives had been changed, and through her work, along with the team of three other missionaries, many Congolese had been brought to the Lord, and some of them were now sharing the gospel and teaching in other remote areas. As she was nearing the end of her testimony, she shared that her daughter Jenny had also been very instrumental in her work with the Congolese people. She had learned their language and worked with many teenage girls and boys, resulting in many teens accepting Jesus as their Lord and Savior. Of course, these children could then share with other children and adults in their families.

In closing, Lou Ann informed the congregation that she had committed to four more years, after which she would return to the states and dedicate her time and efforts to doing God's work. She would let her daughter make whatever decision she felt best in her career. Lou Ann continued by thanking her father and mother and Beaumont Church for letting her share on this Sunday morning. She then handed the mic to CJ.

"Thank you, Lou Ann, for sharing your story. God bless you for what you and Jenny have been doing in the mission field. Folks, a few weeks ago, our pastor gave a sermon on forgiveness. That sermon touched Sara and me a lot. I only pray that after hearing these testimonies today that you will think about that sermon and how it has or will affect your lives going forward. With that and with the pastor's permission, I would like to close this afternoon with a praise song that I believe is fitting. Let's all stand and sing 'Amazing Love.'"

After the closing song, the pastor returned to the stage, thanked the Hilderbrands for their amazing testimonies, and closed in prayer. Although it was 4 p.m., no one was in a hurry to leave the church. The Hilderbrands stepped down from the stage and were mobbed with hugs. Jay and Mick were both seen talking to other boys similar in age. The Beaumont Church had certainly witnessed some amazing testimonies that Sunday, and very few exited the church with dry eyes.

***

That evening, the Hilderbrands all met at Andrew and Jennie's for ice cream and cherry pie. They had also invited Rita Sanchez and Mr. Croft to join them, and both were more than happy for the invite. After ice cream and cherry pie, they all gathered in the family room, and CJ opened the evening in prayer. All in the room thanked God for getting them through their testimonies.

After a time of prayer and thanksgiving, CJ started the conversation. "I'm so proud of all of you. I know it was difficult, but the Holy Spirit really revealed Himself today. I spoke with the pastor afterward, and he had received so many comments on today's sharing by all of you. They couldn't believe how the Lord worked everything out. They all thought you boys were amazing in your willingness to share, and you, Mr. Croft, right under our noses. How did you do it?"

"Well, that was pretty easy, wasn't it, Jay?"

"Yes."

"You see, when I first caught Jay sneaking into the church basement, we made a deal that neither of us would tell anyone about it. Tell them, Jay, what the other condition was."

"I had to attend church every Sunday."

"Shortly after Jay moved in with me, Mick and he met in the balcony of our church, and the rest is history. With can collection, mowing lawns, and just being boys, they weren't around much during the daylight hours. There wasn't much that I had to do to keep it hidden."

"Why, you little devil you," exclaimed Rita. "You always were one step ahead of everyone at the orphanage. Have you pulled any more shenanigans lately?"

The four older Hilderbrands looked at one another with grins and wondered just how Jay and Mick would respond to Rita's question. Jay looked at Mick, who pointed to Jay as if to say, "You tell."

Jay told about his and Mick's failed caper. During the explanation, Rita just smiled and shook her head. Lou Ann and her daughter also found the story quite humorous.

"Lou Ann, can you share some more about life in the Congo?" asked Jennie.

"Working with the Congolese has been rewarding, and it's always exciting when individuals give their life to the Lord, and we have had many people do that."

"What about the food and living conditions?" Andrew inquired.

"It was difficult at first for both of us, but we have been provided with comfortable housing, and the food is different but quite good. We eat a variety of fish, but I think Jenny and my favorite dish is mwambe chicken. It is a dish served with rice and vegetables."

Jay and Mick questioned young Jenny on what games the kids in the Congo played and if baseball was on that list of activities. Jenny explained that soccer was the big sport in the Congo. Although there was an age difference between young Jenny and the twins, they formed a very strong bond.

CHAPTER NINETEEN

*A*ndrew and Jennie were so thankful that Lou Ann and Jenny had committed to staying with CJ and Sara for two weeks before returning to the mission field. It meant that both would be present for the surprise birthday party that the couple had planned for the boys, who would be turning thirteen. Jennie was keeping the event a total surprise and hadn't even informed CJ or Sara.

"Andrew, I so want it to be a special day for our boys."

"I suspect they have never had a birthday party," responded Andrew.

"I doubt so either. They most likely don't even know the date of their birthday. Aside from our family members, who should we invite?"

Andrew pondered the question and replied, "Well, I think the boys would really be happy and surprised to see Rita, Mr. Croft, and I think a real surprise would be Billy."

"That's a wonderful idea, Andrew. Any suggestions for presents for the boys?"

"As a matter of fact, I do have an idea."

"What might that be?"

"Both those boys have bikes that have seen better days. I think a couple of new bikes would be perfect."

"Great idea, Andrew."

"I will go bike shopping and purchase a couple tomorrow. I'll leave them at the store and pick them up the morning of the party."

"Andrew, by the way, we don't have a number for Billy."

"That's okay. I will go by his cart on the way to purchase the bikes. You call all the others and let them know the time. Tell them gifts won't be necessary. Their presence will be enough and greatly appreciated."

Jennie called all the Hilderbrands, Rita, and Mr. Croft. All indicated they wouldn't miss the event for anything. Sara insisted on baking a chocolate cake and accompanying it with ice cream. Rita said she would bring her favorite Mt. Diablo dip and tortilla chips. Jennie told her that would be wonderful.

Andrew arrived at the bike shop, where he purchased two 21-speed mountain bikes. The man at the bike shop said the boys would be happier with mountain bikes rather than road bikes which were usually used for pavement and racing. After leaving the bike shop, Andrew located Billy at his hot dog cart, and, as usual, there were several customers purchasing hot dogs. After the last customer left the cart, Andrew approached Billy.

"Hello, Billy. Looks like you're busy."

"Well, how are you, Mr. Hilderbrand? How are those two boys doing?"

"I'm fine, and the boys are doing well. They are getting excited for the baseball season to start. Billy, I stopped by to invite you to a surprise birthday party for the boys Saturday. They will be turning thirteen. I know Saturday is a busy day for you, but I'm sure the boys would love to see you."

"I wouldn't miss it for anything. What time and what is the address?"

"The party starts at 2 p.m., but we want everybody to show up at 1:30. Here's the address."

***

Jennie saw Andrew pull into the driveway and met him at the front door. "Are the twins home yet?" asked Andrew.

"No, they're still at the park."

"Good, we can talk and not be heard. I got the bikes and stopped to see Billy. He said he wouldn't miss the party for anything."

"Oh, Andrew, that is so exciting. Jay will really be glad to see him. I called everyone, and they all will be here and are really looking forward to the surprise party. That CJ is a real conniver."

"What do you mean?"

"He is going to call the boys Friday evening and ask them if they can give him a hand at the church Saturday around noon. You know our boys. They will do anything for CJ. He will keep the boys busy at the church and deliver them back home a few minutes before 2 p.m. He wants us to pick up all the other family members and have them here by 1:30."

"That sounds like CJ, alright. This is going to be fun."

***

Saturday arrived, and the plans were falling into place like clockwork. Billy arrived at 1:30, and—what a surprise—he had hot dogs, buns, and all the fixin's, enough to feed an army. Rita had brought her Mt. Diablo dip with tortilla chips; they were fabulous and a great hit with the participants. Andrew had hidden the bikes in the garage. Precisely at 2 p.m., CJ and the boys arrived. Jennie opened the door, and as the boys entered, everyone in the room began singing, 'Happy Birthday.' The looks and smiles on the twin's faces would be treasured by all for years to come. This would be a day the boys would never forget.

"Wow, Mick, I've never had a birthday party."

"Neither have I. Can you believe this?"

"You boys stay here a minute, and I will be right back," said Andrew.

Andrew took Billy, and they went to retrieve the bikes. They entered the room, and Andrew spoke. "Here you are, boys. Happy Birthday."

The boys were speechless as they gazed at the new bikes. Jennie was sure she noticed tears in the eyes of both boys.

"These are for us?" asked Jay.

"They sure are," responded Jennie.

"Jay look, they have 21 speeds. I can't wait to try one out."

"You boys can take them for a spin later, but now let's enjoy the hot dogs and tortilla dip. After your spin, we can enjoy chocolate cake and ice cream, thanks to grandma," replied Andrew.

Billy went to the kitchen with Jennie and brought out all the fixin's for his hot dogs. Jennie brought out the Mt. Diablo dip and tortilla chips. This would be the first time that several in the room had ever had one of Billy's hot dogs.

"Billy, I have never had a hot dog that was this good," remarked CJ. "And Rita, your dip is delicious."

Sara, Jennie, and Lou Ann all wanted Rita's Mt. Diablo dip recipe. After everyone had eaten way too much, the boys got to try out their new bikes. Upon returning from a couple of trips around the block, Jay said on behalf of both of them, "These bikes are great. Thank you for getting them for us."

After chocolate cake and ice cream, the party came to an end. They all decided to leave, knowing the boys were anxious to ride their bikes. Before everyone left, they posed for pictures and exchanged hugs. All indicated it was a wonderful party. Special thanks were given to Billy and Rita for providing such delicious food. After everyone had left, the boys were on their bikes, breezing through the neighborhood.

"Andrew, that was a special party. Don't you agree? The looks when the boys saw their bikes were precious. You made an excellent choice."

"It certainly was, and what a surprise when Billy showed up with his hot dogs and all the fixin's."

***

The two weeks had been a wonderful time for all the Hilderbrands. It had been a time of laughter and a time of tears. Lou Ann and Jenny would have loved to stay longer, but Lou Ann knew she had to leave. She hoped to train three new missionaries that were due to arrive there the following month, and she had some pressing commitments to finalize before their arrival.

The next morning, all the Hilderbrands saw Lou Ann and Jenny off. Many tears were shed, but they appreciated the time they had with them and were very proud of their missionary work and commitment to the Congolese people. They all agreed to correspond on a regular basis.

CHAPTER TWENTY

The Hilderbrand household had settled in as a family, and the twins had made the transition well. Jay and Mick, although inseparable, had made new friends with many their age in the church. They, of course, no longer sat in the balcony. They enjoyed the church youth group and its many activities. After their first encounter with Buster, Sara was quite concerned about how they would make friends with the big Doberman. But just as CJ had said, both boys loved the big dog, and a close bond between the boys and Buster had been made.

Jennie and Andrew had discussed with the boys the options of schooling and, for the time being, homeschooled them for two years before high school was decided on. Neither parent was anxious to place the boys into the local schools until they learned just what degree of knowledge the boys had acquired. To their amazement, the boys could have easily entered the public school system immediately. In fact, both were well advanced for their age. The junior high curriculum was almost too easy for the boys, and high school would not be a problem. Jennie and Andrew realized they had been blessed with two very intelligent boys.

Spring was rapidly approaching; it would soon be base-ball season, and Jay and Mick were excited to get on the ball diamond. They were especially anxious to be on the traveling squad that Andrew and Carl had put together.

Baseball wasn't the only activity that would be occupying the boys' time during the spring and summer months. When the word got out around the community and their church family, the boys were being inundated with calls for their lawn mowing services. In fact, CJ and Andrew had purchased a small trailer and two lawnmowing machines for the boys who had, on their own, formed the J & M Mowing service. There was some debate whether it should be J & M or M & J. It was formally decided on by a coin toss, two out of three heads or tails. Jay won, and Mick accepted the results.

The boys had decided on a flat rate to charge their clients. They had received differing amounts from their customers prior to forming their new business. A flat rate of $35.00 was decided on, and no one objected to that price. In fact, most of the customers gave a sizable tip. The monies received were divided equally between the two, as well as the workload. The boys' business savvy was remarkable for thirteen-year-olds.

CJ had agreed to tow the mowers to the various homeown-ers and was thrilled to do so just to observe the boys and the reaction of the homeowners. It also gave him the opportunity to chat with the customers. The fact he knew them all was also rewarding. Oftentimes, those little chats turned into long conversations, which sometimes led to time issues for the next mowing job. However, neither boy complained because CJ was obviously having the time of his life, and he WAS towing the mowers to different sites. He had pretty much stepped down from his business and now had a lot of time on his hands.

Since the lawn mowing business was so lucrative, the boys no longer gathered pop cans in the park.

***

$\mathcal{T}$he big day finally arrived. A three-team tournament had been arranged, and each team would play two seven-inning games against each other. The two out-of-town teams had always been very competitive against Beaumont teams. The twins were excited because the tournament was in Beaumont. Andrew had gotten the word out to the church members, and most were in attendance, as well as Grandma and Grandpa Hilderbrand.

Carl and Andrew had gotten their team huddled up for a pep talk near their dugout. "Well, boys, this is what you have been waiting for. Carl, you choose who should pitch the first game."

Carl flipped a coin. Jay was the winner and was sent to the mound to pitch the first game. Jay breezed through the game and allowed only one hit and no runs. The Beaumont Colts won the game by a score of four to zero. Jay not only pitched a magnificent game allowing two hits but went two for three, including a home run.

After a thirty-minute break, the second game resumed. The Colts took the field with Mick on the mound. He performed just like his brother but only better. Mick allowed one base runner, and that was a result of a walk. This walk prevented a perfect game. The Colts won the game three to zero, and Mick was also two for three with a home run.

After the game was complete, the team was mobbed by the fans, and Jay and Mick's pitching and batting performances were the center of their conversations. The Hilderbrands were extremely proud of their two boys. "I can't believe what I just saw," remarked CJ. "Those boys are destined for baseball careers, or my name isn't CJ Hilderbrand."

Shortly after the second game ended, the two opposing coaches approached Andrew. "Where did you find those two that pitched against our teams today?"

"They are my sons."

"We both thought we had top-notch pitchers, but your boys were outstanding."

"Both of your pitchers did a good job, too," responded Andrew.

"Yes, they are good, but they certainly are not in the same class as those two."

The two coaches left Andrew but didn't go far when he heard several comments.

"Boy, the rest of this league will have a difficult time against those two lads."

"Yes, they will, and I want to find out when they will be playing so I can see just how good they are. The Marino Valley Bandits will be a really good match-up."

"It will indeed. Hopefully, we won't have a scheduled game when they play each other."

"Yes, I hope we don't either. I want to see that game."

Andrew was taking this all in and enjoying every minute of it. He knew they would be playing the Bandits, and fortunately, it was a scheduled doubleheader.

Andrew was again surprised when the local high school baseball coach approached him after the second game. He had been standing close by and surely heard the two coaches that Andrew had been talking to. "Sir, I understand you're the father of the two boys that pitched for the Beaumont squad today."

"Yes, that is correct. I'm Andrew Hilderbrand and our two sons Jay and Mick pitched today."

"Well, I'm Lester Burton, and I'm the high school varsity baseball coach. By the way, I have been visiting with your granddad, CJ, during the two games. He has filled me in on some of the backgrounds of your two sons, which is rather amazing, I might add. As I understand, they are currently being homeschooled."

"Yes, that is correct. At this point, my wife would like to do homeschooling for two years before their high school years begin."

"That's good to know. I was concerned."

"What do you mean concerned?"

"Well, I'm not sure what policy our school takes on home-schooled students and their eligibility for school sports. What I saw today and who I know is coming out for varsity base-ball this year, those boys are already more talented than any pitchers we have returning this season. I assure you I will be watching them every chance I get during this year. Incredible what I saw today, and I compliment you on two very talented ballplayers. Not only can they pitch, they can also hit."

Andrew had a grin from ear to ear as he responded, "Thanks for your compliments and concerns. I will let the boys know that the high school coach saw them play today."

"Thanks, and I assure you I will be keeping my eye on those two."

The season went by way too fast, and the Beaumont Colts traveling team went undefeated with a record of ten wins and no losses. Each boy won five games, and both were credited with pitching perfect games, a rare accomplishment for any pitcher regardless of age.

Those two perfect games just happened to be against the Marino Valley Bandits, which were picked to win the league. The two coaches that Andrew and Carl's team had played the first of the season just happened to be in attendance. Andrew had spotted them in the stands, and both had stood up and given Andrew the thumbs up and hollered out, "Way to go, coach. You knocked off the number one team. Your boys were unbelievable." They, like Beaumont, had been undefeated.

CHAPTER TWENTY-ONE

$\mathcal{A}$ lot of excitement was present on this Sunday morning, as it would be a special baptism service at Beaumont Calvary Chapel. Both Jay and Mick had accepted Jesus as their Lord and Savior, and today they were going to be baptized. The fact that Lou Ann's young daughter Jenny was responsible for bringing the twins to the Lord was special to the Hilderbrands. The two weeks before leaving for the Congo, young Jenny and the twins had spent a lot of time together. The boys had asked a lot of questions about the Congolese youth and were quite interested in their knowledge of Jesus. This opened the door for Jenny to witness to the boys. She shared her testimony and the importance of making a public statement of faith through baptism. It was unfortunate that she couldn't be present that day.

Neither parent had pushed the boys into baptism. They wanted that decision to be made by Jay and Mick. However, they did explain what baptism was all about and its importance. The twins had told Andrew and Jennie that young Jenny had told them about baptism, but neither parent was sure how much detail had been shared.

The baptismal request had been made the previous Sunday, and today the sanctuary would be filled. Andrew would assist the pastor with the ceremony, and, of course, Jennie, CJ, and Sara would be very proud.

After the service that evening, a celebration dinner was planned at CJ and Sara's, which would certainly include pork chops, fried chicken, and all the trimmings. Dessert would follow with ice cream and cherry pie.

The following evening after their family Bible reading, Andrew turned to Jennie and asked, "Do you have any regrets about not pursuing your career in Marine Biology?"

Without a moment's hesitation, Jennie replied, "Absolutely none. These boys have fulfilled my absolute dreams, and God has so richly blessed us. I wouldn't trade what we have now for anything in the world. We all have Jesus as our Savior, and I'm positive our names are in God's Lamb's Book of Life."

"Yes, we can, praise God for all that has happened, and today's service makes that even more special." Andrew continued, "There is one thing that I remembered today."

"What is that?" questioned Jennie.

"Remember, we told Rhonda at the orphanage we would let her know when and if our boys and us were brought together. We haven't done that yet, and I keep hearing this voice inside me telling me to do so. I have her number, and now is the time to make that call." Andrew went through his phone log and remarked, "Here it is, Rhonda Dupree." Andrew dialed the number.

"Hello," Rhonda answered.

"Hello, is this Rhonda?"

"Yes, this is she."

"Rhonda, this is Andrew Hilderbrand."

"Oh yes, hello, Andrew. How are you and Jennie doing?"

"We are both fine, and I apologize for not calling you sooner. I want you to know that both boys are with us, and today they were baptized."

"Well, praise God. I have prayed for you two every day, and yours and my prayers have been answered. The Lord never ceases to amaze me. In fact, your calling me is a miracle in itself because you know what?"

Andrew was silent for a moment and then responded, "What?"

"I was just getting ready to call you. You told me when we met a few weeks ago that Jennie may not be able to deliver any children because of a medical problem."

"Yes, since Jennie has been told it would not be wise to deliver another natural child, we have put that on hold for the time being."

"I'm so sorry to hear that, but the reason I was about to call you was my remembering your desire for more children, and would you consider adoption?"

"Yes, I'm sure if the opportunity were available, we would consider adopting. Of course, Jennie and I would discuss and seek God's will. I get the feeling you're about to tell me something that may require a lot of prayer."

"Well, I just might. Last week a set of identical twins were brought to our orphanage. They are three years old and are darling little girls. You and Jennie talk it over and pray about it. I want these girls to go to a loving Christian home, and I know after meeting you two that you would be exactly who I would love to see these girls go to."

"Thank you so much, Rhonda. Hang on a second while I get Jennie on the phone."

Jennie got on the phone and had a long conversation with Rhonda. Rhonda filled Jennie in on all the details that she hadn't shared with Andrew about the girls. "Oh, Rhonda, thank you so much for thinking of us. Andrew and I and, yes, our boys will discuss and do a lot of praying. This is so exciting, and you know what? I think God is about to perform another miracle."

EPILOGUE

The successful removal of the birthmarks on the twins brought closure to their anxieties, allowing them to participate in activities they had not previously participated in.

Jay and Mick had no difficulties adjusting to the public school system and were co-valedictorians of their senior class at Beaumont High School.

Perhaps the highlight of their four years at Beaumont High School was their participation on the varsity baseball squad. That squad was undefeated and won four consecutive state championships. The four years of being undefeated were attributed to Jay and Mick, who pitched every game during that time. Needless to say, both boys were heavily recruited by several major college universities.

The most rewarding was not the victories but the satisfaction of knowing the six Hilderbrands attended every game. *Six*, because now the boys were the brothers of adorable twin sisters.

But on this day, there would be eight Hilderbrands and two Summers in the stands. Jennie's parents had retired from the mission field and were now living in Beaumont. Lou Ann and Jenny had returned from their Congo mission. All ten would be watching Jay and Mick playing in their first college career games. Jay would be pitching for the UCLA Bruins, and Mick would be the starter for the USC Trojans.

Earlier, a charred letter was referred to that Jennie missed while walking through the remains of the orphanage. That letter read as follows:

Dear Jennie and Andrew:

A severe storm shut down all means of phone contact. We also have had some severe electrical issues at the orphanage that I feel are unsafe. I have tried to call but no service. I moved the twins to nearby orphanages until the electrical problems are fixed. Please don't be disappointed with me for doing this, but I felt it best for the twins.

Love and may God bless you,
Maria